COOL BREEZE

A NAUTICAL NOVEL

BY

ED ROBINSON

D1518447

Cool Breeze is dedicated to the real-life Holly Freeman. Rasta-hippie Holly has inspired me with her free living lifestyle and thirst for adventure. May her sails always be filled with wind.

One

Captain Hard-Ass was pounding conch with a stainless steel hammer. A large black woman was sitting on a cooler, swatting flies. I'd come to shore to get a beer or three, but the bar was closed.

A couple of locals were standing around, with bottles of Kalik in their hands.

"Where'd you get the beer?" I asked.

They pointed at the woman on the cooler.

"Good afternoon," I said to her. "Can I get a cold Kalik, please?"

She rolled her eyes and rose very slowly. I apologized for making her get up. She ignored me as she opened the cooler and grabbed a bottle out of the ice. She started looking around for a bottle opener. She acted like she hadn't seen it in days. My cold beer was warming by the minute. Finally, she located it. She handed me the open beer.

"Three dollars," she said.

I handed her a five. She took it with no thought to giving me my change. I waited. I drank my beer. We stared at each other until the beer was empty.

"You owe me two bucks," I said.

She rolled her eyes again and mumbled something under her breath. She dug around in an old cigar box and came up with the two dollars. I added a one and asked for another beer. At least she was already standing. I would have hated to make her get up again.

It was a typical day in Morgan's Bluff. In a few short days, I'd come to hate the place. It was a ghetto harbor. The biting flies were enough to drive a man insane. The beach was lined with the wrecked hulls of unfortunate vessels that broke free during various storms. *Leap of Faith* was the only boat anchored in the bay. I needed to get her out of there soon, but I didn't know where to go next.

Originally, I'd planned to go home to Pelican Bay on the west coast of Florida. I'd headed north from the Dominican Republic after parting ways with my most recent love interest. Holly had headed south for the exotic ports of the Caribbean Sea. After running hard for a few days to clear the Turks and Caicos and the southernmost islands of the Bahamas, I changed my plan. Traveling alone was tiring. I decided to take it slow. I wanted to visit some of the anchorages I'd never been to. Morgan's Bluff was one of those places.

I'd been kicking around the Exumas, Eleuthera, and the Abacos for months. I'd lost sight of going back to Florida, until then. The bad ju-ju that floated around Andros was enough to make me remember home.

"Got a big blow coming in tonight," said Captain Hard-Ass. "If it starts coming out of the north, you'll be in trouble out there."

"The weather service didn't seem to think it would be all that bad," I said.

"Weather service don't know shit," he said. "You can trust Captain Hard-Ass. It gonna blow real hard late tonight. I can feel it in my bones. First it storm. Then it blow."

"Thanks for the heads-up," I said. "I'll throw out a bunch of extra chain."

I went back out to the boat to prepare for whatever weather may come. I didn't know if the old man was full of shit or not, but better safe than sorry. The wind was out of the east at a comfortable ten knots. My transom was pointing towards a concrete sea wall with two sunken boats laying alongside. I didn't like the looks of that, so I pulled up anchor to reposition the boat. I found a nice, clear sandy spot in ten feet of water in the center of the harbor. I was well protected from any wind direction, except the north. North winds turned this place into a death trap, as evidenced by the wrecks on the beach. I let out one hundred feet of chain. A ten-to-one ratio would hold me in all but hurricane force winds.

I cooked up a snapper that I'd caught on the reef that morning. I had a few beers after dinner. I laid off the rum. I wanted to be sharp if things got hairy. I turned in at ten, hoping that the old man was wrong.

He wasn't. The storm came in around midnight. Lots of lightning came with it. A thunderclap directly overhead woke me. I sat on the back deck and watched the light show until the driving rain forced me back inside. Then the wind came. At first, it was only blowing thirty knots, but it was indeed out of the north. It quickly increased to fifty knots. If it continued like that, I was in trouble. It took a while for the seas to build, but build they did. Soon I had eight foot waves rolling under my hull. Cabinet doors swung open and canned goods rolled around the salon floor. Books flew off the shelf. I'd taken the time to make sure I was properly anchored, but I hadn't secured the interior of the boat. I staggered around inside locking cabinets and putting breakables in safe places.

It was impossible to stand without holding on to something. I sat on the settee and looked out the port windows. I focused on the red and green lights that marked the entrance to the commercial harbor. There was no room for me in there. I was suddenly jealous of the few boats that had taken refuge there before the storm. The anchor was holding, but it was being sorely tested. I wanted to put out more chain.

I carefully made my way forward to the bow. The waves were tossing *Miss Leap* around like a kid's fishing bobber. The bow was rising and falling a good ten feet. I couldn't release the bridle that I used on the chain. The tension was too great. The seas were too tall. I'd either fall overboard or crush my fingers in the windlass. I gave up on that idea, and retreated back inside. I spent the night watching those red and green lights. At one point, the boat came down off a wave so far that the transom went under water. It quickly drained out the scuppers, but I was concerned. I'd never seen that happen before, and I'd been through some rough stuff. It was too dark to see the wreckage on the beach. I was happy for that. The rain let up but the wind continued. It blew a sustained fifty knots all night long. I watched the red and green lights all night long. I added chafe protection to the dinghy painter. I dozed off briefly but was wide awake at daybreak. It was still blowing. The anchor was still holding.

The first indication that it was easing off didn't come until after noon. I guessed that the wind was down to thirty knots. I was tired from lack of sleep. I was hungry. I was also tired of being on a violently rolling boat. I took a wild dinghy ride to shore, just to put my feet on dry land. I looked back out at my boat. It was still bucking like crazy. I figured that if my anchor held all night in fifty knots, it would continue to hold now. I took a nap on a bench in Regatta Park before walking up to the bar.

The bar was still closed. The large black woman still sat on her cooler. I didn't feel like aggravating her for a beer.

"Man, what kinda anchor you got?" asked Captain Hard-Ass. "Your boat be jumping around like a bucking bronco."

"Forty-four pound Bruce," I told him.

"I want to know what kind of drugs he's on," said another local. "Crazy riding out a storm like that out there."

"I warned him yesterday," said Captain Hard-Ass.

"Yes you did," I said. "I'll buy you a beer, but you'll have to wrestle with her yourself."

I handed him a twenty and told him to get his buddy a beer too. The large black woman was much nicer to them than she'd been to me. I got the impression she didn't care for white people. That hadn't been the case anywhere else in the Bahamas, but Andros was unlike the other islands. It was a wild place, with rough terrain. It was made of solid rock and inhabited with biting flies and tough people. They were the descendants of runaway slaves from the United States. Their ancestors had launched small boats from places like Key Biscayne. They rowed and sailed across the Gulf Stream, landing on Andros. They survived the wilderness and made a life here somehow. You couldn't help but admire them for that. As for me, I couldn't wait to leave.

As I got in my dinghy to head back to my boat, I noticed a sailboat in the harbor. It was anchored way too close to *Leap of Faith*. I had been the only boat out there. There was no reason to anchor so close. I cursed whatever asshole had intruded on my personal space, and headed out into the bay. The wind had given up. The seas were almost calm. As I drew closer, I got a better look at the intruder. I couldn't believe my eyes.

It was *Another Adventure*. Holly was in the harbor.

Two

There were four people onboard Holly's boat. They were a ragged looking bunch. As I approached they hollered and blew conch horns to greet me. I tied off and climbed aboard. I was immediately greeted with a big hug from Holly. She was the last person I expected to see there. I was speechless.

We both spoke at the same time.

"What are you doing here?" we asked.

"I'm taking a slow round-a-bout way home," I said. "I haven't made it back to Florida yet."

"I went back to Marathon," she said. "I picked up this crew and we just got back. We heard we can check into Customs at the bar here."

"The bar's been closed," I told her. "Introduce me to your crew."

A little guy with the most gnarly dreadlocks I'd ever seen stuck his hand out. He called himself Rabble. He had a raccoon skull woven into his hair. The backbone of some unidentified animal adorned another dread. The whole mess of matted hair resembled a wet dog that hadn't been groomed in years. He stood a few inches over five feet tall. He was thin but wiry. His long pants were filthy. He wore no shirt. He had assorted black tattoos everywhere.

His girlfriend was named Darla. Her dreads were much tamer. She was dirty too, with hairy armpits. She looked very young, maybe twenty years old. Rabble looked to be about thirty.

I turned to Holly and the guy standing beside her. He had his arm around her waist. He was also very young. I guessed young twenties. He wore board shorts like Holly's with no shirt. His abdomen was tattooed with the words *Hakunah Matata*. He introduced himself as Simba.

"Do you have a real name, son?" I asked Simba.

"Tim," he said, shaking my hand.

"Okay, Tim," I said. "I'm not calling a grown man Simba."

"No problem," he said.

The entire bunch was all smiles. They were a boatload of hippies on another adventure. I was curious how and why Holly had ended up there with them. Last I knew she was traveling south from the Dominican to points unknown, by herself.

"I got lonely pretty fast," said Holly. "The romance of the high seas wore off and I went back to Florida. I met Simba and these two in Boot Key Harbor. I'm going to show them the Bahamas, like you did for me."

"This dump ain't the Bahamas," I warned her. "There's nothing here but bad vibes."

"It's just our first stop," she said. "We sailed straight through from Marathon and spent the night on The Banks."

"You were anchored out on The Banks in that storm last night?" I asked.

"It sucked real bad," she answered. "We got up this morning to pull anchor, and it was gone."

"You lost your anchor?" I asked.

"Yup, the rode cut right through during the night," she answered. "We were adrift and didn't even know it."

"It was no picnic here either," I said. "But if you drag here you end up wrecked on the beach."

"I'll keep that in mind," she said. "But we just want to check in and move on."

"I'm moving on too," I said.

"Come with us," she offered.

"I don't know, Holly," I said. "I'm getting pretty close to Florida. I should just go home, finally."

"What's a few more months?" she asked. "It'll be fun."

She looked me in the eyes. I looked into hers. There was something there, but I didn't know what. This Simba kid was her boyfriend apparently. Why did she want me tagging along?

"I've told my crew all about you, Breeze," she said. "They're probably tired of hearing about our adventures. It would be great if you could join us as we make some new memories."

"Which way you heading?" I asked.

"The Exumas," she said. "We want to hop our way to Georgetown before we head back to Florida."

"You going to sail straight through from here?" I asked.

"That's the plan," she said. "First stop Allan's Cay."

"I can't make it there straight through," I said. "I'll stop in West Bay first. I can make it in two days."

"We still have to check in with Customs," she said. "Plus we want to take a look around."

"Nothing to see here," I said. "But suit yourself. I'll leave in the morning. Meet you at Allan's in a few days."

"That's awesome," she said. "It's so good to see you, Breeze."

She wrapped her arms around me and squeezed me tightly. She whispered in my ear.

"I thought I'd never see you again."

Breeze Junior took note of her hard body. Unlike her crew, she appeared to be clean and well groomed. She smelled nice. I separated from her before things got out of hand.

"Great to see you again too," I said. "Nice to meet your friends."

I backed away but our eyes held their gaze for a few more seconds. I avoided eye contact with Tim while I climbed back down into my dinghy. I waved goodbye and made my way back to my own boat.

I grabbed a beer and a bottle of rum. It was going to take some serious drinking to figure out this new turn of events. Two months prior, I'd watched Holly sail over the horizon. I figured she was gone forever. I was determined to go back to Florida, but had dragged my feet and ended up in Morgan's Bluff, for no particular reason. Now Holly was there too, with a boyfriend, and a crew of dirty hippies. There was absolutely no good reason for me to travel with them to the Exumas. Why had I agreed? I knew the answer to that. It was to be around Holly, boyfriend or no boyfriend. Florida would still be there when I got back.

I continued to ponder until my brain got a little fuzzy. I didn't like the looks of that Rabble character, but I'd gotten no particular bad vibe from him. Darla seemed to just be along for the ride. She had a vacuous air about her, not a serious thinker. Rabble was dominant in their relationship. Holly held that role over Tim. He looked at her with puppy-dog eyes. He seemed earnest enough, eager to please. I'm sure some psychiatrist could figure out why she'd chosen someone so young after having been with me, but I had a hard time accepting it. The boatload of them made me feel old. Eventually, the rum won out over serious thought and I turned in for the night.

I was ready to roll in the morning, but there was one small problem. My boat wouldn't start. The starter seemed to be engaging, but the engine just went clunk. I checked the voltage to the starter. It was fine. I scratched my head and stared at the engine for a minute. That didn't cause it to start. I didn't know what the hell the problem was. It had never done this before. Holly's voice came over the VHF radio.

"I thought you were leaving today," she said.

"Boat won't start," I replied. "Not sure what the problem is."

"You want a hand?" she asked.

"Sure," I said. "If you think you can help."

Holly and Tim paddled over in separate kayaks. I explained what it was doing and what I'd checked so far. She had me try to start the engine. Clunk.

"Shit, Breeze," she said. "I think you got water in the engine."

"What?" I said. "How's that work?"

"You went through that storm and all that wind," she said. "The motion can cause a siphon effect. Exhaust elbow fills up. Water's got to go somewhere. It backs up into an open port through the exhaust manifold. Water in a cylinder I bet."

"That sounds bad," I said. "What do I do now?"

"Bring me your tools," she said. "I can fix it."

"No shit?" I said. "Amazing."

"It's not fixed yet," she said. "But I was quite the gearhead before I was a sailor."

I watched as she got down in the bilge and started turning wrenches. She removed all the injectors. She tried to turn the engine over by hand, but couldn't budge it. I took over. I was able to move it about a quarter turn. We all heard water sloshing in the engine. Her diagnosis had been correct. I was having a hell of time trying to turn the engine over. Tim offered to give it a try. No. I wouldn't let him show me up. I couldn't have some young buck show me how strong he was in front of Holly. I strained with all I had. The engine rolled over and water poured out through the exhaust. I thought my back would break.

"We've got the compression off of it now," I said. "Can't I use the starter to turn it over?"

"That's probably not a bad idea," said Holly. "Try it."

I held the stop button at the same time I pushed the starter button. The engine turned freely for a few seconds.

"That should do it," she said. "Let me put it back together."

Tim got down in the bilge with her and together they reinstalled the injectors. She explained what she was doing to him, teaching him. He listened intently and asked good questions. I felt a bit useless as I watched a hot chick and her young boyfriend work on my engine. When they were done, Holly told me to fire her up. It started immediately, like nothing had ever been wrong. Holly held her arms in the air.

"I win!" she said.

I hugged her and the three of us cheered. I tried to pay her. She refused. Just helping out a friend.

They left and I pulled anchor. I still had plenty of time to get to West Bay before dark. I marveled at my luck. Running into Holly here was pure coincidence, but she ended up saving my ass.

Thanks, Holly.

Three

It was less than thirty miles across the Tongue of the Ocean to West Bay. Soon after losing sight of Andros, I could make out the tall buildings of Paradise Island and Nassau. I'd avoided those places like the plague. I didn't go to the Bahamas to see casinos and urban sprawl. There wasn't much to do or see in West Bay, but it was a beautiful anchorage to spend the night in before moving on.

I left for Allan's Cay bright and early. By luck I arrived at slack tide. This made it much easier to enter the cut and get anchored properly. The current really rocks through there. Anchors drag. Boats get damaged on the rocks. I didn't like it much as an anchorage, but that's where Holly said we'd meet. I went to visit the iguanas on Fowl Cay before starting my happy hour. I kept an eye out for *Another Adventure*, but it didn't show. It wasn't there when I woke up in the morning either. They should have arrived by then. Had they dumped me?

The current made me nervous. I was uncomfortable there. Holly was a no-show. When slack tide returned, I decided to leave. The boat wouldn't start. It sounded exactly the same as it had in Morgan's Bluff. I pulled out my tool bag and got to work. I watched Holly closely enough to know what to do. I busted a few knuckles and got grease all over me, but I got it started.

Highborne Cay was less than an hour away. I'd be more at ease there, while I figured out what to do next. I found several mega-yachts anchored near the south end of the island, close to the marina. I came in to their north to anchor off the beach there. I was looking for a good spot when I saw them. *Another Adventure* was anchored further off the beach. I passed them by and went closer in. I saw Rabble and Darla on the sand. They waved. I have to admit, I felt relief to find them again.

Holly came up in her dinghy soon after I set the anchor.

"I called you on the radio a bunch of times late yesterday," she said.

"I didn't have it on," I admitted.

"Leave it on channel 72," she said. "We need a way to stay in touch."

"Will do," I said. "What happened?"

"It was dark when we got here," she said. "I didn't want to try to get in over there in the dark."

"It sucks as an anchorage anyway," I told her. "Nothing there but iguanas."

"Rabble wants to catch one and cook it," she said.

"They're protected," I said. "Not a good idea."

"He's all in to that survivalist stuff," she said. "Living off the land."

"Plenty of fish to eat," I said. "Don't let him get you into trouble down here."

"Frank is here," she said.

"Frank who?" I asked.

"From Boot Key," she said. "On the little sailboat, *Tilly*."

"Okay, I remember him," I said. "He's a long way from home in that little boat."

"We should get all of us together for a bonfire," she said.

"Not here," I said. "Those folks up there at the marina will run us off. Norman's Cay would be good. It's not far."

"Is that where the sunken plane is?" she asked.

"Yup. Good snorkeling spot," I answered.

"We want to check that out," she said. "Let's spend a day here and then we'll all go down together."

"Sounds good," I said.

She went off to join the rest of her crew. Highborne Cay is an upscale marina. I guessed they wouldn't be too happy to see the likes of Rabble come ashore. I should have warned Holly. Then again, she chose her mates. I wasn't in charge of her anymore.

I decided to turn on my handheld VHF. I turned it to channel 72. I put my base unit radio on channel 16. There wasn't much chatter. I got a beer and propped my feet up on the transom. The water was a beautiful blue and crystal clear. I watched Rabble and Darla return to *Another Adventure*. He got a fishing rod and casted over the side. At least he wasn't cooking an iguana.

Later that afternoon, I heard Holly on channel 16. She was hailing a passing fishing boat. He switched her to channel 68. I followed. She wanted to know if it was legal to keep a nurse shark. Rabble had one hooked and had it at the side of the boat. The fishing boat captain explained that although it was indeed legal to keep, the locals wouldn't be too happy about it. Nurse sharks are considered pets in the Exumas. The locals feed them at the fish cleaning stations. At Staniel Cay, you can get in the water with them and pet them. I'd never had the urge to pet a shark, but that's just me. She thanked him and signed off.

I watched as Rabble and Tim pulled a large shark up over the rail and into the cockpit of *Another Adventure*. A few hours later, Holly invited me over for a shark meat dinner. I didn't really care to eat a nurse shark, but I accepted her invitation. When I got there, the carcass was still in the cockpit. It had been butchered thoroughly. There were blood and guts everywhere. I wasn't squeamish about fish blood, but Holly's boat was a mess. I'd have never allowed such a thing on *Leap of Faith*. The guys had cut the shark up into steak-sized slabs. One of those was thrown on the grill. Frank came over, but he couldn't stand the mess. I begged off too. I told them I had something thawed out that I really needed to cook before it went bad. I left the hippies to their nurse shark steaks and went back to my boat. I took three beers to clear the smell out of my nostrils.

The next day, three boats left Highborne bound for Norman's Cay. I went first. Holly followed me. Frank brought up the rear. We all anchored up close to shore, tucked in behind a jagged point of rock. The day was nice and the beach beckoned. Five of us scoured the island for driftwood. We got a nice pile built up for a bonfire after dark. I decided to find the bar. Rabble, Darla and Frank followed. It was called MacDuff's, and it was very nice. Much too nice for Rabble and Darla. The cheapest thing on the menu was a twenty-five dollar cheeseburger. Rabble and Darla disappeared. Frank and I bit the bullet and ordered the burger. Our beers cost seven bucks apiece. It was a good burger. I would have gladly paid ten bucks for it.

After dinner, we joined the hippies on the beach. Tim had a guitar. Darla had a hula hoop. Rabble had some paraphernalia whose purpose I couldn't determine. We got a nice fire blazing and passed around a bottle of rum. More shark steak was cooked over the fire. I tasted a chunk. It was inedible. I tossed it on the fire. Darla's hula hoop was ignited by Rabble. She spun and danced with flames spinning around her. Tim started strumming the guitar. Rabble pulled out his equipment. He lit the end of a rod and used rum to breathe fire. It shot out away from his mouth a good five feet. My mood mellowed with the rum and the fire. I was impressed by his fire breathing ability.

After a few more stunts, he extinguished the flaming rod in his mouth. Tim's guitar sounded pretty good. Holly's pretty face glowed with the reflection of the flames. Darla spun around and around. A billion stars twinkled above us. There was no moon. There were no other boats or people within twenty miles. Just me and the hippies, drinking rum and playing in the sand.

Sometime near midnight, I heard Holly squeal. She'd wandered off down the beach by herself. What she discovered was that our dinghies had floated off the beach. She grabbed hers. Mine was just a few yards offshore. Frank's was nowhere to be found. She hopped in her little boat and went off to search for it. It refused to be found. She went to her big boat to get a spotlight. Off she went into the night. Eventually, she gave up. Frank's dinghy was history. That was enough to harsh our mellow. We put the fire out and called it a night. I dropped Frank off at his boat on the way out.

I had honestly enjoyed the night, but it ended on a sour note. It felt like a bad omen. My engine problem needed to be resolved. Frank was without a dinghy. The hippies would be eating foul-tasting shark meet for another week. There was something not quite right with the atmosphere surrounding our little adventure, but I couldn't put my finger on it. I tried to work the problem through in my head, but fell asleep before reaching any conclusions.

The light of a new day didn't change things. I still felt something wasn't quite right. I'd trusted my life to my instincts many times over the years. I observed people. I watched their eyes and their body language. I listened intently to what they said. I determined strengths and weaknesses. I stayed aware at all times. I catalogued my observations in my mind for future use. It had kept me alive so far. Rabble had given me no indication that he was a bad guy. In fact, he was reasonably intelligent and inquisitive. I sensed no malice, but still, he made me uneasy somehow. None of the others put off a bad vibe of any kind. I knew Holly intimately. Tim seemed like a nice kid. I believe he was sincere and straight-forward. Darla was just Darla. She had little impact on the situation.

I kept coming back to Rabble. I had no evidence, but I couldn't resist blaming this disturbance in the force on him. It was like he was blocking my sixth sense. I needed to get away from him to clear my mind. Getting away from him meant getting away from Holly. I decided to call a group meeting to discuss our near-term plans.

We all met on *Another Adventure*. The mess had been cleaned up, but the boat was still dirty as hell. Holly and crew wanted to see a lot of stuff. The wanted to go diving, hiking and kayaking. Frank wanted to find a new dinghy. I wanted to fix my engine. In the end, we decided that Frank and I would make a beeline for Georgetown. We hoped to get whatever we needed there. Holly and crew would island hop their way south until they met back up with us there. I'd get away from Rabble, but still be able to see Holly again. It seemed like a good plan. I got another hug from Holly before departing. Tim didn't seem to mind.

Frank and I left the next morning for Big Majors. *Goodbye Holly. See you soon.*

Four

Big Majors is the home of the famous swimming pigs. Frank wanted to go see them up close. I could have cared less. He tried to beach his little sailboat, but grounded it on some rocks instead. I used my dinghy to tugboat him off the rocks and into deeper water. Instead of anchoring, he tied off to my boat. This was a practice I wasn't fond of. We had a few beers and discussed the rest of the trip.

We left early the next day bound for Little Farmers Cay. The winds were calm and the Exuma Banks were flat. It was our last stop before Georgetown. We went out through the cut the next morning. The current carried *Miss Leap* along at over eight knots. Out in the Sound we had a light chop, nothing we couldn't handle. It was a long, boring day. We made Elizabeth Harbor well before dark. I chose to anchor off Stocking Island, at Sand Dollar Beach. Frank anchored nearby.

Over the next several days, Frank made a general nuisance of himself. Every time I got in the dinghy to go someplace, he had to tag along. I took him to the grocery store. I took him to the bar at Chat-n-Chill Beach. I took him with me everywhere. Each morning he would get on the radio, looking for a new dinghy. Finally, he realized he was being a pain in my ass. He moved his boat close to the town's dinghy dock. Each morning he'd flag someone down for a ride. Each afternoon, he'd bum a ride back to his boat from the docks. He spent his days in town trying to track down a dinghy. None of those offered were right for him. They were either too expensive, too big, or in bad shape. I thought that beggars shouldn't be choosers, but he saw it differently.

Meanwhile, I was attempting to figure out what was causing the problems with my engine. I got lots of advice from fellow cruisers, but no real solutions. I spent too much time sitting on a bar stool at Redboone's Café. There I was, stuck in the far southern Exumas for no particular reason other than the chance to spend time with Holly. She wasn't there yet. Frank was a much less attractive option to spend time with. I kicked myself for agreeing to this trip. I should have just gone home to Florida. Then again, what if my engine failed out there on the Gulf Stream?

I picked people's brains until I found someone who really knew what he was talking about. Rodger was on a big trawler named Rolls Doc. He'd been a Rolls Royce mechanic his entire adult life. He had Lehman engines like mine. We discussed all the circumstances that led up to the problems. He thought about it briefly, asked a few more questions, then he took me down into his engine room. He pointed at a hose that carried seawater through the oil cooler and into the exhaust elbow.

"There's your problem," he said. "Pull that hose off. If the water is right up to the top of it, that's what's happening."

I did as he suggested. The water was indeed right up to the top of it.

"What do I do now?" I asked.

"For the moment, keep your seacock closed while you're anchored," he said. "I'll order you a vented loop. That will take care of the problem."

The air freight company only brought packages in to the airport once a week. We'd just missed them. I waited another week for the part to come in. Then I had to hire a broker to import the part for me. They charged me fifty-five dollars, filled out all the paperwork and sent me to the Customs office. At Customs, I handed the stack of papers to the agent. She took them from me and sat down at her desk. She watched TV. I stood there for a few minutes until someone told me I could take a seat. I sat. I sat for thirty minutes while the Customs agent watched Dr. Phil. Finally, she took the paperwork over to a clerk, who called my name. I paid her eighteen bucks to cover the VAT tax. She stamped my paperwork and I returned to the broker. He checked that everything was complete.

"Come back around three o'clock," he said. "I haven't been to the airport yet."

Back to the bar I went. You do a lot of waiting in the Bahamas. The concept of Island Time is no myth. Nobody really gives a damn about your problems. They certainly aren't in hurry. I saw a familiar face across the bar. I'd seen him back in Marathon. He was on a bar stool then too.

"The last time I saw you, you were sitting on a bar stool," I said.

"Yea?" he said. "Where was that?"

"The Lobster House in Marathon," I told him.

"Hell, I practically lived in that bar," he said. "Only good thing about that damn town."

"I seem to remember you were pretty down on the locals in the harbor," I said.

"I sailed around the world," he said. "I traveled the Caribbean and most of South American. I'd been gone for ten years. I thought I wanted to go home. After a month in Marathon, I said screw this. Now I'm gone again."

"Where you headed?" I asked.

"Wherever the wind blows me," he said. "South most likely."

"Good luck to you," I offered.

He grunted something I didn't understand. He wasn't a real friendly guy, but he was someone to talk to besides Frank. I hoped Holly would arrive soon. Not that I didn't waste away most of my days, but I was getting restless just sitting there doing nothing.

As far as I knew, Holly was only bringing her crew as far south as Georgetown. Maybe we could all travel back to Florida together. Maybe I'd get to see a lot more of her. I wasn't even sure why I wanted that. She was with someone else. We'd decided it would never work out between the two of us. I'd tried to put her out of my mind after we parted, but when I saw her again, all those familiar feelings rushed back in.

My thoughts went back to the enigma that was Rabble. My gut told me he was bad news. It wasn't just his appearance, I didn't really care about that. I live and let live. No, it was simply a gut instinct. He'd cause trouble somewhere along the way. His ultimate intentions weren't good. It didn't really feel like danger, just a nagging suspicion that he was up to no good. I vowed to keep a close eye on him when they arrived.

Time went by and the part I needed to cure my engine woes arrived. Still no sign of Holly. Rolls Doc left the harbor. Frank kept more to himself. Someone had lent him a little boat. He had a means of transportation without bothering everyone in the harbor. I spent my days sitting in the water drinking beer, or watching the bikinis at the Chat-n-Chill. I spent my nights reading. My life was a far cry from the action and adventure that those novels portrayed. Doc Ford was chasing bad guys in a South American jungle. Jesse McDermitt was chasing bad guys in the Florida Keys. I was getting fat and lazy, drinking too many beers in the Bahamian sun.

I took to hailing *Another Adventure* on the VHF radio every afternoon. I got no response for a week. One day out of the blue, I heard Holly hailing me.

"*Leap of Faith, Leap of Faith. Another Adventure,*" came the call.

"You've got *Leap of Faith,*" I said. "Are you in the harbor?"

"Just entering now," she said. "Where are you anchored?"

"Sand Dollar Beach," I told her. "Plenty of room."

"See you shortly, Breeze," she said.

"Welcome to Georgetown," I replied.

She came in under sail. Her boat passed twenty yards off my stern. Her crew greeted me with hollers and conch horns. She stood at the helm wearing a bikini top and her ever-present board shorts. She picked an open spot, dropped her sails, and glided to a stop. The anchor went over and she settled in like a pro. She was a true sailor, and I admired her abilities. I wasn't so sure about her judgement when it came to picking friends, or crew in this case. She was a trusting person. She wasn't judgmental about your appearance or choice of lifestyle. She gave you the benefit of the doubt. She assumed the good in people until they proved otherwise.

That's where we differed. I assumed the bad in people until they proved otherwise. I didn't trust people until they proved trustworthy. Holly had won my trust. The rest of her crew had not.

Holly and Tim paddled over for Happy Hour. I was glad to talk to them without Rabble present. After exchanging pleasantries, I got right to the point.

"How's things going with Rabble and Darla?" I asked.

"We've had enough of them, Breeze," said Holly. "I really need to get rid of them."

"What's up?" I asked.

"They aren't pulling their weight. They're making a mess of my boat," she said. "They are ungrateful, freeloading, slobs."

"That's too bad," I offered. "I didn't get a good vibe from Rabble. Any signs of him causing trouble for you?"

"I don't think he's a bad person," she said. "He's just more trouble than he's worth."

"How are you going to get rid of them?" I asked.

"I guess take them back to Florida," she said. "We need to get fuel, food and water first."

"How long you sticking around here?" I asked.

"Maybe a week or two," she said. "We just need some time apart from them."

"I'm ready to head back whenever you are," I said.

"You want some crew?" she asked, laughing.

"Hell no," I said. "And I know you wouldn't do that to me."

"I was just joking," she said. "It's my problem."

"Have you given them any indication that you're sick of them?" I asked.

"Maybe a little," she said. "Trying to keep it mellow."

"I don't trust Rabble," I said. "Watch him, especially if he knows you want to dump him."

"I don't know what trouble he could cause," she said. "He needs us to get home."

"Just be careful," I said. "Tim? Are you paying attention?"

"Yes, sir," he said. "Keep an eye on Rabble, don't trust him."

"Can you take him, if it comes to violence?" I asked.

"I'm not a fighter," he said. "But he's a pretty small guy. I think I can take him."

"I know I can kick his ass," said Holly. "I'll knock him out and throw him over the side if it comes to it."

"Just be careful," I said. "Stay aware. Don't let him take advantage of you. If you need my help, just ask."

"Thanks, Breeze," said Holly. "But I think we can handle it."

"We'll be fine," said Tim.

I couldn't shake the feeling that something bad was about to happen. I couldn't imagine what trouble Rabble could cause, short of going full-blown psycho, but all the alarms were going off in my head. At least they'd made it to Georgetown. If something did go wrong, I'd be there to help, however I could.

Five

The five of us played in the water, digging up sand dollars and harassing star fish. Rabble and Darla were still wearing the same clothes. He had on his filthy long pants. She wore her nasty cutoff shorts. Who doesn't bring bathing suits to the Bahamas? Both Holly and Tim wore board shorts that looked relatively clean. I cringed every time someone called Tim, Simba. It was a silly hippie thing.

Tim had turned out to be a nice guy. He was smart and friendly. He obviously adored Holly. I tried not to let it bother me when they got affectionate with each other. Good for him. Holly was a hell of a catch.

I let a week pass before starting to hint that I was ready to leave. Holly and crew still hadn't filled up with fuel or water. They were eating canned goods or fish that they caught. They snorkeled the reefs. They explored the town. They didn't seem to be in any hurry to leave.

One night after dark, I was sitting on the back deck with a cold beer. I could hear them arguing. I couldn't make out the words. I just heard raised voices. I detected no signs of violence, so I didn't interfere. Eventually, they settled down. I sat and listened for another hour. I heard nothing else, so I went to bed.

In the morning Holly called on the VHF. She sounded frantic.

"Rabble is gone," she said. "He took all of our money."

"What did he leave in?" I asked.

"The two-seater kayak," she said. "Darla is gone too."

"I'll go to town," I said. "See what I can find out."

"Thanks, Breeze."

I jumped in my dinghy and hurried to the docks. The kayak was tied up on the outside pier. I jogged up the ramp to Redboone's. It was too early for drinkers, but two taxi drivers sat on benches outside the café.

"Either of you see the dreadlocked dude this morning?" I asked.

"I took him and the girl to the airport first thing," one of them said.

"Can you run me out there now?" I asked.

"Sure thing, mister," he said. "Twenty dollars round-trip."

I gave him a twenty and he opened the passenger door for me.

"My name's Clifford," he said, handing me a business card. "You ever need a ride, you call me."

"What time does the plane for Florida leave?" I asked him.

"One to Key West is already gone," he said. "Fort Lauderdale leaves at noon."

I doubted that Rabble would just sit around in the airport for hours. He'd have taken the first plane out. Still, maybe I could pick up a hint or a clue there. Clifford dropped me off at the entrance to the one-terminal airport. I asked him to wait.

I went up to the empty ticket counter.

"Good morning, sir," said the attendant. "What can I do for you today?"

"A young couple," I said. "Long straggly dreadlocks. You can't miss them."

"They boarded the early flight, sir," she said.

"For Key West?" I asked.

"That's correct," she said. "Almost on the ground by now."

"Thanks," I said, handing her a twenty. "Did you happen to overhear anything they said that might help me find them?"

She took the twenty. She looked around to see if anyone was watching or listening. No one was paying any attention.

"They argued," she said. "Not loud, real quiet like."

"What about?" I asked.

"He was sending her away. Making her go back home," she said. "Michigan I think."

"Was she upset about it?" I asked.

"She cried," she said. "But he was real cold to her. He didn't show any emotion at all. Just told her how it was going to be."

"Did they have any luggage?" I asked.

"Just backpacks," she answered. "They carried them on."

"Okay, great," I said. "You've been very helpful. I appreciate it."

"You have a nice day, now," she said.

Clifford was waiting at the curb.

"Ain't none of my business," he said. "But did you find the hippie kids?"

"They're gone," I said. "Flew to Key West."

"I had a bad feeling about that dude," he said. "He done something bad ain't he?"

"He robbed a boat in the harbor," I said. "Friends of mine."

"It's usually the locals looking to steal," he said. "Boat folks don't steal from each other."

"No, not normally," I said.

"What are you going to do now?" he asked.

"I don't know Clifford," I said. "But if I need a ride I'll be sure to call you."

"You tell your friends too now, hear?" he said.

"Will do, Cliff," I said. "Thanks for the ride."

I took the dinghy back out into the harbor and went to Holly's boat.

"They flew to Key West," I told her. "He's ditching Darla, sending her home."

"He took every cent we had," she said. "Singles, change, everything."

"I'll spare you the lecture," I said. "But I warned you. You should have secured your cash somehow."

"There's four of us living on a sailboat, Breeze," she said. "Everybody knew where it was."

"We need to stay calm and come up with a plan," I said. "Let's all just relax and put our heads together."

We sat in the cockpit. Tim brought us bottled water. Holly was taking long, deep breathes. Tim massaged the back of her neck.

"Where would he go from Key West?" I asked.

"He's got a sailboat in Boot Key," said Tim.

"What is it?" I asked. "What's the name of it?"

"It's old, needs work," he said. "It's called *Winter's Dream*."

"Any significance to the name," I asked.

"A retired New York cop owned it," said Tim. "Before he could finish restoring it, he died. His name was Bob Winter."

"So you know some of Rabble's history?" I asked.

"We were friends," he said. "This is my fault."

"You can't blame yourself," said Holly. "Neither of us thought he do something like this."

"Breeze knew," said Tim.

"Breeze isn't like the rest of us, Tim," she said. "His mind is like a computer. He's always calculating. He's got a lot of experience dealing with criminal types."

"He warned us," said Tim. "We should have taken him more seriously."

"It's not the first time that I screwed up by not listening to him," she said. "You'd think I would learn."

Tim looked at me with question marks in his eyes.

"Cuban patrol boat, Coast Guard, close call," I said. "Long story."

"I'd like to hear it sometime," he said.

"We can tell you over some cold beers after this is all over," I said. "So he's got a boat in Marathon."

"He left it anchored down near Dockside," said Tim. "Some locals are keeping an eye on it."

"Does it run?" I asked. "Can he leave on it?"

"It overheats," he said. "But it runs for twenty minutes or so before it gets hot. It's got sails."

"Can he run away in it, Holly?" I asked. "I mean is he capable of sailing it?"

"We've been teaching him," she said. "He's got the basics down. He's no dummy."

"So he's in Key West by now," I said. "He can take the shuttle to Marathon this afternoon."

"And we can't do shit about it," said Holly. "We're dead broke."

"I've got money," I said. "If you've got a plan, don't worry about money."

"I don't have a plan," she said. "That's your territory."

"You two can fly out in the morning," I said. "Catch him before he can set sail."

"I don't want to leave my boat here," she said. "Unless you're going to sit here and babysit."

"I'd rather not," I said. "Next suggestion?"

"You fly out and catch him," she said. "It's what you do."

"Then my boat is left here," I said. "You know how I feel about my boat."

"We'll stay here and watch it for you," she offered. "If you can spot us some money for food."

"If he takes off on his boat, I'll need a boat to track him down," I said. "Where would he go, assuming he can get the boat out of the harbor?"

"He used to talk about the Everglades all the time," said Tim. "He was obsessed with going there. He was on his way there when he started having his engine problem."

"Did he figure out why it was overheating?" I asked.

"Blown head gasket," said Tim. "He never had the money to fix it."

"He does now," I said. "But it will take a few days."

"What about weapons?" I said. "Will he be armed?"

"He's anti-gun," said Tim. "He carries that machete with him all the time though."

"What are you thinking, Breeze," asked Holly.

"He knows you can't come after him," I said. "He took all your money. No reason for him to think that I'd come after him. He's doesn't know me. So he takes his time. He fixes his boat. He gets some groceries. He'll need fuel and water. Maybe it will take him a week."

"How does that help us?" she asked.

"I can be there in five days," I said. "If he gets out of there before then, he won't have gone far."

"And you'll have your boat to hunt him down," she said.

"It's a long shot," I said. "But he is very recognizable. He'll turn up somewhere."

"What do we do?" asked Tim.

"I'll give you money or food and fuel," I said. "Start making your way back to Florida. If he's not in Marathon or the Everglades, we'll both look elsewhere."

"I really hate to be in your debt," said Holly. "We've been down that road before."

"We'll find him," I said. "We'll get your money back. We can square up then."

"I used to wonder how you got all these missions," she said. "Now here I am handing you another one."

"If you live enough life," I said. "Shit's gonna happen."

"And shit always works out, right?" she said.

"You've learned well, young grasshopper," I said, in my best Chinese accent.

Six

Rabble had taken almost twelve thousand dollars. I had to argue with Holly, but she accepted ten thousand from me. That way, if and when I recovered the stolen money from Rabble, I wouldn't have to get it back to her. We'd be even. If I failed, I'd be out ten grand. I had a mission.

Holly and Tim still had to get fuel and food, but they'd trail behind me by a few days. After their bad experience, they were ready to go back to Florida anyway. I sat down with my chart books to figure out the quickest route to Marathon. I'd have to head north first, to get onto the Banks. I could veer south to Riding Rock and cross to Marathon from there. If all went well and I really pushed it, I could make it in four days. That is, if the weather cooperated. I had plenty of fuel and water. I spent the night getting mentally prepared. I could feel the juices beginning to flow. My senses were heightened. I always got this way when starting a new mission. It was my drug.

I pulled anchor at first light. The seas were calm and I made the sixty mile trip to Big Majors in just over nine hours. The next morning I left well before sunrise to cross the Exuma Banks to New Providence Island. I used every minute of daylight before pulling into West Bay. It was a long day. I drank two beers and turned in early. I still had a long way to go to get to Marathon. I didn't know what would happen when I got there. Either Rabble would still be there or he wouldn't. Maybe he ditched the boat and flew off to some unknown destination, never to be seen again. I decided to stick with following up on the information that I had. I'd successfully resolved this sort of manhunt before. My instincts told me I'd find him.

I was up at four the next morning. My mind was racing with the anticipation of the chase. The anchor was up and *Leap of Faith* was underway by five. If I stayed on the recommended routes of travel, there was nothing to hit. I'd be okay in the dark for a few hours. I made the Northwest Channel and turned to the west. Eventually, I veered southwest towards South Riding Rock. I didn't make it before dark, but I got the anchor down by nine that night. Next stop Marathon.

I'd had superb weather so far. I'd been lucky. I needed one more day of calm seas. I had no way to get a weather report out here. I'd been reading the sky, watching the clouds, and studying the sea state. There had been no indication of any approaching weather system. I was stuck under a high pressure system that was providing fair weather. I said a quiet prayer to the weather gods to give me one more day.

I was up early again and underway before daylight. The Atlantic was flat. Not a drop of coffee was spilled as I watched the sun come up behind me. It felt good to be on the move and to have a purpose. It was a strange niche in life, but this is what I was born for. The open sea put a smile on my face. The hum of the diesel engine comforted me. The sound of water swishing along the sides of *Miss Leap's* hull was music to my ears.

I thought about Rabble. He was too small to be a physical threat, at least in hand to hand combat. He didn't like guns. He carried a machete. I tried to visualize how it might go when I confronted him. My first option was to carry a gun. Never bring a machete to a gunfight. If he resisted I might be forced to shoot. Then what? Leave his body for the gators to clean up? I wasn't sure if I could sleep at night if that scenario played out. My next option was to take him down before he could draw his weapon. That required a situation where stealth could be utilized. It wasn't likely to happen while boarding a small sailboat. So how do I defend against a machete attack?

I mulled over the idea of fabricating some kind of small shield. I considered some sort of leather sheathing for my arms. I thought about how he might swing it at me. It had to be overhead or sideways. If he missed he'd be left in a very vulnerable position. I'd grab his arm to control the weapon and proceed to administer an ass-whooping. To help kill the time, I ran dozens of different scenarios through my mind. In each one, I ended up holding the machete while standing over Rabble's inert body. I felt confident that I could handle the little man. I just had to find him first.

I returned my attention to the weather. A slight drop in temperature alerted me to possible changes to come. The wind, which had been nonexistent, came to life in the form of a light breeze. It didn't stir up any waves. It just put a ripple on the water's surface. There were some low clouds over the east coast of Florida. There was no sign of a thunderstorm. *Leap of Faith* chugged along like she always did. Her engine purred like a contented kitten. We pushed on across the cobalt blue expanse of the Gulf Stream.

Late in the afternoon the wind increased. It stirred up a small chop at first, which gradually grew. I could see Sombrero Light in the distance. I needed another hour to get inside the reef. The safety of Boot Key Harbor was another hour beyond that. The low clouds shot up into the atmosphere. Their bottoms flattened out and turned black. The wind and waves were coming off the land straight towards me. I lost some speed as the bow starting climbing up and falling down the waves. I watched lightning strike over Florida Bay. It didn't look like I'd make it inside the harbor before all hell broke loose, but I pushed on.

I was running along the shoreline of Boot Key when the bottom fell out. I was so close, but it was raining so hard I couldn't see a damn thing. The wind was now over thirty knots. I pulled back on the throttle and turned the bow towards land. The island provided a small amount of shelter. I dropped anchor and prepared to wait out the storm. There was no point in trying to navigate the narrow entrance channel and pick up a mooring ball during a storm. There was nothing else to do but wait.

As soon as I sat down in the salon, I realized how tired I was. I'd covered over three hundred nautical miles in four days. I laid down right there on the settee and fell asleep. When I woke up, it was well after dark. The storm had long since ended. I decided to just sit tight for the night. Rabble could wait another day, if he was still around.

Marathon City Marina managed the mooring field in Boot Key Harbor. I waited for them to open before pulling up anchor.

"Marathon City Marina, Marathon City Marina, Leap of Faith on channel 16," I hailed.

"Leap of Faith," they replied. "Acknowledge and switch to channel 14,"

"Roger, One Four," I said.

I switched the radio channel.

"Leap of Faith on fourteen," I said.

"Welcome back," came the reply. "How long will you be staying with us this time?"

"Just a day or two," I said. "Any ball will be fine."

"Q-4 is available," the voice said.

"I'll take it," I replied. "I'll be in to settle up as soon as I get settled."

I slowly made my way into the narrow entrance channel. I passed by Pancho's and Burdine's. I went through the bridge to nowhere. There was a motley collection of junk boats on my starboard side before I cleared the bridge. The anchorage inside the bridge was fairly full. I could have anchored in there with them, but I wanted to go to the marina and ask around about Rabble. I could also take advantage of the showers by paying for a mooring ball. I needed a good, long shower by then. I picked up the mooring ball, put the dinghy down, and took off for the docks.

The usual crowd of beer drinkers was hanging out at the tiki hut.

"Anyone seen Rabble?" I asked.

Maresa was sitting at the picnic table. She was the first to respond.

"The dreadlock dude?" she asked.

"Yea, that's him," I said.

"He was around here for a few days," she said. "But I think he's gone."

"Anybody else talk to him?" I asked the others. "Where did he go?"

I got blank stares and shoulder shrugs. They didn't know or they weren't telling. I went into the office and paid for one night.

I took a dinghy ride to the anchorage down by Dockside. There were two sailboats with someone aboard. I approached *Rogue*. The guy on board eyed me suspiciously.

I'm trying to find the dreadlocked guy that was here on *Winter's Dream*," I said.

"He left," was the response. "Left yesterday."

"Did he say where he was going?" I asked.

"Didn't talk to the dude," he said.

I motored over to *Bamboozle*. I vaguely remembered its occupant.

"You Steve?" I asked.

"That's right," he said. "Who's asking?"

"Breeze," I said. "I've seen you around the harbor some."

"How can I help you?" he asked.

"I'm looking for Rabble," I said. "Dreadlocks. Was anchored here."

"He pulled out yesterday," he said. "Showed up a few days ago, did some kind of work on his boat and rolled out."

"Any idea where he was headed?" I asked.

"Everglades," he said. "Said he was going to live off the wilds way up in the Glades. I told him he won't last a week with those mosquitoes. Crazy fucker."

"Thanks, Steve," I said. "I appreciate the help."

"Why you looking for him?" he asked.

"He robbed some friends of mine," I said.

"Call the cops, man," he said.

"Happened in the Bahamas," I said. "I want to catch up to him before he's too far gone. No time for police reports and do-nothing cops."

"Well, good luck, I guess," he said. "I never did trust that dude."

"Good instincts," I said. "I owe you for the info."

"Nah, man," he said. "No skin off my back."

"Okay, later then," I said.

"Take it easy," he said.

My own instincts had been correct. He was hiding in the Everglades on his sailboat. Finding him in the thousands of square miles of swamp might have seemed like an impossible task, but there was only one entrance into the Glades that could support a deep draft vessel. He was in Little Shark River. I was only a day behind, but I needed to pick up provisions and take that long-overdue shower. I didn't want to get stuck in Little Shark without enough food and water. It was a desolate place. The bugs drive most people out after one day.

I got my shower. I got my groceries, including lots of bug spray. I called a cab so I could stock up on beer and rum. I ate a burger at Burdine's before returning to my boat before sunset. I sat with a cold beer and watched her go down. All around me the sounds of conch horns filled the air as the sun blinked out.

I woke up ready to go. After coffee I motored over to the fuel dock and topped off the diesel and water tanks. Back out the channel I went. I turned north and went under the Seven Mile Bridge. *Miss Leap* and I skirted a few shoals and wound our way up into Florida Bay. Thankfully, the commercial lobster season was closed, so the bay was free of traps. I punched in a course and engaged the autopilot. *I'm coming for you, Rabble.*

As I got further north in Florida Bay, I noticed the water clarity was off. There was a lot of dead, floating sea grass. It didn't look healthy. When I'd left south Florida, the ecosystems of both coasts were a mess. Constant discharges from Lake Okeechobee were wreaking havoc on the delicate balance of nature in both the Caloosahatchee and St. Lucie watersheds. Now I was witnessing the downstream effects. The Everglades were starved for fresh water. Florida Bay was suffering as a result. Man, in his infinite wisdom, thought he knew better than Mother Nature or God.

Draining the swamp had once been all the rage. In the interest of agriculture and development Man had redirected the historic flow of his greatest resource, water. Big Sugar had planted its roots deeply in the new dirt below the dyke at the southern end of the big lake. Big Sugar had also planted its money deep in the pockets of politicians all across Florida and in Washington. Big solutions were needed, but Big Sugar stood guard against any steps that might be taken to hurt its continued financial success. Meanwhile, the taxpayers subsidized the entire process. It was maddening to consider just how far we'd gone to screw things up in south Florida. I stopped thinking about it.

I turned my attention back to the task at hand, finding Rabble. I'd find him. I'd find Holly's money. I'd wipe my hands of the whole mess and go back to Pelican Bay. This mission had given me the reason I needed to head back home.

I made Cape Sable by mid-afternoon. I rode along the park boundary markers until the entrance to Little Shark River came into view. I turned inland, picking up the green marker at the river's mouth. I saw no boats. There is a small, round basin just inside that makes a good anchorage for one or two boats. It was empty, so I chose the center of the basin and dropped my anchor. I put a bridle on the chain and backed down. The hook set firmly in the dark mud. The bugs were already on me. I retreated inside to slather down in bug spray.

Once I was covered in DEET, I went back outside to look around with my binoculars. I saw no sign of a sailboat. I'd hoped maybe I could spot a mast sticking up above the mangroves, but I had no such luck. I was here for the night. If Rabble came down the river to leave, he'd have to come right past me. If he was upriver, I'd find him with the dinghy, eventually.

I spent the night sweating and swatting mosquitoes. Little Shark was a godawful place. My discomfort was plenty of incentive to end this thing quickly. I'd make Rabble pay for robbing Holly. I'd also make him pay for forcing me to come to this hellhole. The buzzing in my ears kept me awake for hours, but I finally dozed off. My dreams were full of bugs, alligators and dreadlocked demons.

As soon as I woke up, I reapplied bug spray. My coffee tasted like DEET. The interior of my boat was a toxic fog of pesticides. The exterior was blackened with a million of the little bastards. Despite the heat, I put on long pants and a long sleeved shirt. I wrapped a bandana around my neck and doubled up on the bug spray. I headed up the river in search of a sailboat. I had extra gas, extra bug spray, and an itching to bring about some justice. It was not going to be a good day to be Rabble. I was in a foul mood. Mercy was not on my mind.

He was way up in the maze of mud and mangroves. He'd anchored on one side of the river, with both a bow and stern anchor out. He had long lines tied to thick mangrove roots, holding him close to shore. I thought those lines were a good way for critters to board his vessel. Maybe he wasn't as a smart as he thought he was. My four stroke outboard was quiet, but not so quiet that he wouldn't hear me coming. Any visitor approaching in this wilderness would alert him instantly. There was nothing I could do about that. I'd just have to jump aboard and hope for the best.

I came up alongside but didn't see him. Maybe he was ashore or off exploring. I climbed into the cockpit. All of my senses were on guard. I saw a kayak tied to the boat on the side closest to shore. He had to be onboard. No one swims in the Everglades. The companionway was open except for a screen covering the opening. I could see just a small portion of the interior. No sign of Rabble. If felt like a trap. He was most likely standing down there with his machete raised, poised to hack me up. It was decision time. I could go in slowly, talk calmly and try to bring a peaceful end to the situation. I could bust in hard and fast, try to surprise him with sheer violence and bravado. I could sit and wait him out, in the cloud of mosquitoes that now surrounded me.

The last option was quickly ruled out. I decided to let him think I had peaceful intentions. I'd wait for a chance to switch up and smother him with knuckles, elbows and knees.

"It's Breeze, Rabble," I said. "The gig is up."

"I don't think so," he said, from somewhere deep inside.

"Just give me Holly's money and I'm out of your hair," I offered.

"Good luck taking it from me," he replied.

"I'm going to come in nice and slow," I said. "We'll work this out. Easy now."

I took two steps towards the companionway. I heard and felt him come forward. The boat moved almost imperceptibly, but I sensed it. It was time. I launched myself through the opening feet first. I grabbed a handrail on the way down to keep from falling. Just as I landed, I heard a whiz and a thud right next to me. Rabble was holding a spear gun in both hands. He'd already fired. The spear lodged into a bulkhead behind me.

"Shit," he said, reaching for his machete.

He wasn't quick enough. I was on him before the blade cleared its scabbard. He went down under my weight. His machete arm was pinned between us. I gave him two quick rights to the jaw and a left to his nose. He let go of his weapon and tried to fight back.

Bright red blood poured from his nose and lip. He'd need some dental work later. He poked at my eyes and scratched my face. I put a knee into his chest and tried to push him through the floor. I grabbed a handful of dreads intending to smash his skull on something. He head-butted me good and hard. I hadn't seen that coming.

I had blood in my eyes. I wasn't sure if it was his or mine. I still had a good grip on his hair. I used it to hold his head back while I drove my fist into his face a dozen times. He was still scratching and clawing so I drove the back of his head into the floor twice. That was enough. He gave up. His body went limp and he laid his arms back on the floor. I stayed wary in case it was a trick. I grabbed a piece of rope, rolled him over and tied his hands behind his back. I leaned him against the wall, seated upright. He spit blood on the floor.

"Where's the money?" I asked.

"Holly's not screwing you anymore," he said. "What do you care?"

"She's my friend, asshole," I said. "No where's the money?"

"Pretty nice piece of ass for an old guy like you," he said.

I kicked him in the side of his head. His lights turned out. I'd had enough of the ignorant little son of a bitch. I wasn't sure if my rage was due to his insult of Holly, or calling me old. It didn't matter. I'd find the money myself. I knew a bit about hiding cash on a boat. He'd managed to make my foul mood even worse, so I wasn't careful in my search. I ripped out drawers and dumped their contents. I tossed the cushions, ripped a few open just for spite. Eventually, I found a small hatch in the floor that provided access to the bilge pump. There it was. A small metal box sat in an inch of black bilge water. It wasn't exactly a novel hiding place.

I checked on Rabble. He was still out. I sat and counted the contents of the box. It contained just over ten grand in assorted bills. I started to take it all, but changed my mind. Holly owed me ten grand so that's all I took. I left him with a few hundred bucks. He might decide to become a model citizen after today. He'd need to eat.

I sat and looked at Rabble. The blood in his beard and dreads had turned black and thickened. He looked very small in defeat, but he'd put up a good fight. The spear gun was unanticipated. If he'd have been a better shot things would have turned out quite differently. He didn't keep his cool. He rushed the shot. He should have remained calm, controlled his breathing, and stuck me like a grouper on a reef. Instead, I had the money. All he had were some broken teeth, a busted lip, and a big knot on his head.

I took the spear gun along with three extra spears. I left him his machete. He could figure out how to cut his hands free when he woke up. I'd be long gone. I went back to my boat, fired up the engine and headed out into the Gulf. I was ten miles out before my adrenaline levels returned to normal. My mission was accomplished.

Seven

Soon after I calmed down, I realized that I had arranged things so that I wouldn't see Holly anytime soon, if ever. Why had I done that? I'd been so focused on finding Rabble that I'd let the mission take precedent over our friendship. It wasn't the first time I'd done that. Something about having a purpose gave me tunnel vision. I was real good at concentrating on the job. I wasn't so good at concentrating on relationships.

So there I was, out there in the Gulf all alone. The satisfaction of teaching a crook a lesson wore off quickly. What now? I resigned myself to being alone. I was good at that. I ran northwest for twenty miles to avoid the Cape Romano Shoals. Eventually, I turned north and east, angling towards Marco Island. I could see the tallest buildings of the island from fifteen miles out. The water out here was still clear. It had a blue-green color to it. It couldn't match the clarity of Bahamian waters, but it was still pretty.

Instead of anchoring in Factory Bay like I usually did, I decided to go up the old ICW. I dropped the hook north of Marco in a nice little cove just off the channel. This was an anti-Rabble move, just in case he tried to find me. I developed an adrenaline hangover around sunset. I decided to help it out with a few shots of rum.

In the morning I continued north until I reached Wiggin's Pass. I reentered the Gulf there and ran along the shoreline towards Fort Myers Beach. The further north I went, the worse the water quality became. By the time I neared the entrance to Matanzas Pass, it was a horrible dark brown. It smelled. It was thick with solid matter and foam. Once again, I was disgusted with just how stupid we were as a species. I didn't believe that any fish could survive in those foul waters. It was clear that the Lake O discharges were still ongoing.

I took a mooring ball towards the back of the west field. I sat and looked at the shrimp fleet and the pirate ship at Salty Sam's. There was a guy up on the bridge holding a sign of some sort. I guessed he was protesting for clean water. Some of the cars honked their horns at him. I recalled that old TV spot where the Indian had tears in his eyes because of a polluted earth. Fort Myers Beach could have used a crying Indian up on that bridge.

Robin came by in his skiff. I got caught up on the lives of my backwater friends. One-legged Beth was in the hospital with some sort of viral infection. Robin had broken things off with her months ago. She wouldn't stop the drinking and the drugs. She'd let herself go pretty badly, he told me. Robin and Diver Dan were no longer partners. Robin had started his own dive business. He was calling himself The Dive Guy. He said that the barnacles were growing so fast that there was enough work for two divers in the harbor. Even then they could barely keep up. The nutrient rich slurry coming down the Caloosahatchee River was a boon to the dive business, even if they had almost zero visibility. I worried that one of them would catch some sort of disease swimming in that gunk every day.

I found out that my old friend Jamie had moved ashore. His boat was still on a mooring ball. His health had deteriorated to the point he couldn't get in and out of his dinghy. His girlfriend had helped him make the transition to life on land. I was sad for him. He was a longtime seafarer. I doubted being a landlubber would agree with him.

Robin took off just after dark. I turned in early. The condition of the water, along with the condition of my friends, had depressed me. I decided to leave the very next day. I knew that Pelican Bay had the power to restore my soul.

I started feeling better as I passed under the power lines that ran from Pine Island to Sanibel. The water cleared up near Captiva Pass. Dolphins greeted me near Cabbage Key. I wasn't an Indian, but I had a tear in my eye as I entered Pelican Bay. I'd been gone for far too long. It felt like home. I had a special attachment to that place. It had sustained me when I had nothing. It had taken me in and hidden me from the world. I'd grown dope on Cayo Costa. I'd cooked up homemade rum on Punta Blanca. I'd ridden out storms, and marveled at the rainbows afterward. I'd caught plenty of fish, played with the manatees, and laid on the beach. It cured whatever ailed me. I wasn't sure exactly what was ailing me at that moment, but I knew I could fix it there.

I anchored in a familiar spot in the southern end of the bay. *I had no fussy neighbors. I could fish off my front porch. I had the beach in my backyard. I was Smiling Out Loud.**

(Taken from a Jim Morris song)

After a few days of lounging around doing nothing, I decided to get in better shape. I didn't work too hard at it, but I did a little jogging, a little swimming, and some calisthenics. I laid off the rum. I ate fresh fish. I worked on my tan. I wasn't preparing for anything in particular. I didn't need another job anytime soon. I just felt the need to be ready for anything. It was a crazy world out there. I could avoid it for a time, but I'd need civilization sooner or later. You never knew when some crazed shooter would show up at the grocery store, or an exploding Mohamed would pick your bar to win his seventy-two virgins.

I got a little leaner and a little meaner. I hated push-ups and sit-ups, but I knocked them out every day. I was swimming about a mile at a time. I never was a strong swimmer, but it was a great way to firm up my aging body. I was running maybe three miles a day in the sand. I felt good.

While taking care of myself, I neglected my boat. The Bahamian salt and sun had been hard on the teak and finish. I needed to redo the cabin top and toe rail, but I didn't have the supplies. I decided to go to Punta Gorda. I could walk to West Marine from Laishley Park Marina. I pulled up anchor and made the familiar trip up Charlotte Harbor.

"Laishley Park Marina, Laishley Park Marina, *Leap of Faith* calling."

"Switch to channel one nine, captain."

"Roger, one nine."

"Welcome back, Breeze," said Rusty. "It's been a while."

"Thanks, Rusty," I said. "I need slip for a few days, maybe a week."

"I'll put you in D-5," he said.

"Roger, D-5," I answered.

After I got tied up I went to the marina office to pay the tab.

"There's been two people here looking for you," said Rusty.

"They weren't Russian were they?" I asked.

"No, they weren't," he said. "One of them was your hot lawyer lady friend. She left her card and asked that you call her right away."

"Who else?" I asked.

"He said you were old buddies," he said, handing me another business card.

It was Jimi D. The card had a local number on it. He couldn't be in Florida, could he? Taylor wanted something from me too. I didn't really care to get involved with her again, but I was curious. Jimi D. and Taylor. Taylor and Jimi D. I smelled trouble. These two cards had trouble written all over them. I thanked Rusty and started walking to West Marine.

Everything was good as long as I stayed away from people. As soon as I had set foot on land, people starting complicating things. Neither Taylor nor Jimi were calling to catch up on old times. They wanted me for something. Both of them were selfish, self-centered sorts. They wouldn't be doing me any favors. They wanted me to do a favor for them. My curiosity ate at me while I picked up what I needed from West Marine. It continued to nag me as I walked back to the marina.

Finally, I gave in. I'd call them. I didn't have to cooperate. I'd just find out what was going on, see where it led. I knocked on my neighbor's boat, Mojito. Tina met me with a big smile.

"Oh, Breeze," she said. "It's so good to see you. Where have you been for so long?"

"Bahamas, mostly," I said. "Good to see you too. Can I borrow your phone for a minute?"

"Sure, come on in."

I wasn't quite ready to talk to Taylor yet. I called Jimi first.

"It's Breeze," I said. "I'm on a borrowed phone. Make it quick."

"We need to meet," he said.

"Where are you?" I asked.

"Close," he said. "But no one knows I'm here. Let's keep it that way."

"You're crazy to come back here," I said.

"I think I can make things right," he said. "But I need your help."

I liked Jimi D. I didn't trust him, but I liked him. There were certain to be strings attached to his offer to make things right. I decided to hear him out.

"Where should we meet?" I asked.

"Leave the marina and walk up river on the Harbor Walk," he said. "There's a bench before you get to the hospital. I can be there in ten minutes."

"This better be good," I said.

"Judge for yourself," he said.

I hung up and gave the phone back to Tina. I wouldn't call Taylor until I heard what Jimi had to say.

"Thanks," I said. "I may need to use it again later."

"Anytime," she said.

Then she hugged me and kissed me square on the lips.

"Where's Herb?" I asked.

"He's helping a friend work on his boat," she said. "He'll be gone all day."

She had a very mischievous look in her eye.

"Uh, I gotta go," I said. "Catch you later."

"Don't be a stranger," she said.

I'd run with thieves and drug dealers, but I was not going to mess around with a married woman. Everyone has a line they won't cross. That was mine. It was a ten minute walk to the meeting spot. Jimi was already there when I arrived.

"You look good, Breeze," he said. "All tan and fit and whatnot."

"What's this all about Jimi?" I asked. "I can't believe you're in Florida."

"I want to pay back all the money I took," he said.

"First off, that's hard to believe," I said. "Secondly, what do I have to do with it?"

"I'm serious," he said. "I can pay it all back."

"Why do I think there's a catch?" I asked.

"It's like this," he said. "I took all the money I stole, and turned it into a lot more money."

"Sounds like you," I said.

"I can pay them all back and still have a cool million for myself," he said.

"Why do you need me?" I asked.

"I wouldn't last five seconds with one of those guys," he said. "I'd have a bullet in my head before I could explain."

"I don't even know who they are?" I said. "What am I supposed to do?"

"Taylor does," he said. "She'd jump at the chance to facilitate a deal."

"She wants to talk to me too," I said.

"Do you know what about?" he asked.

"No idea," I answered. "I chose to talk to you first."

"I'm flattered," he said. "I'd choose seeing Taylor over meeting me any day."

"I'm not sure I want to talk to her at all," I said.

"I need you to talk to her," he said. "You can help me work this whole thing out."

"Where are you hiding?" I asked.

"I got a boat," he said, smiling. "I want to live like you do. I want you to show me the ropes."

"Where's it at now?" I asked. "Someone will eventually recognize you."

"It's down at the Riviera," he said. "Trust me. No one goes down there."

"You're staying at Cat Shit Key?" I asked. "That place is disgusting."

"That's why I need you to teach me," he said. "Show me how to get into Pelican Bay. Show me where else I can hide out."

"First things first," I said. "Let's see if we can get you out of trouble."

"You'll talk to Taylor," he asked.

"I'll talk to her," I answered.

"Awesome," he said. "Call me when you know something."

"Lay low in the meantime," I suggested.

"If you get me out of this mess, I'll owe you big time," he said.

"We'll see," I said. "Now beat it, before someone sees you."

They say it takes money to make money. Jimi had just proven that to be true. His million bucks wouldn't do him any good if he was dead though. He used to be legit. Taylor sent some of her more unsavory clients his way. They trusted him with their investment accounts. They needed a nice little offshore tax shelter for ill-gotten gains. He robbed them all. He used their money to make money. Now he wanted to pay them back. I didn't know these men. I only knew that the money wasn't earned honestly. At least one of them was willing to kill his accountant over the loss. Taylor had used me to track him down. Instead of turning him over, I'd gotten Jimi to pay off his debt. I helped the intended victim escape certain death. I hadn't forgotten Taylor's role in that mess. She'd used me.

I tried to suppress the memories of making hot, sweet love to her. I needed to be cold and calculating. I couldn't let her beauty cloud my judgement, like I'd done in the past. She'd certainly been cold and calculating when she sent me to arrange a man's murder.

I waited a day before calling her. I'd had enough for one day. I also wanted to make sure that Tina's husband was around when I borrowed her phone again. I took the stairs to the upstairs bar at Laishley Crab House. I drank beer and looked down at the marina. There was a time when I'd be paranoid about someone finding me. I didn't have that problem these days, but old habits were hard to break. I made careful observations about the boats and anyone I saw on the docks. It was a bluebird day in south Florida. Nothing seemed amiss.

Eight

I thought about just walking to Taylor's office, but I hadn't seen her in over a year. We spoke over the phone while I was in the Bahamas. The conversation hadn't ended well. I'd been pissed that she got me involved in something evil. I was mad at her and mad at myself for being so stupid. I'd basically put an end to our relationship, with a great big exclamation point. Now she wanted to talk. She was probably in trouble. I doubted that she'd seek me out to give me good news.

If she needed help, I'd give it if I could. We were tied together in each other's lawlessness. She'd helped me bribe a judge, after all. Her connections with the seedy side of the south Florida judicial system had helped to keep me out of jail. My friend Captain Fred's political connections had aided us both in the subsequent fallout and investigation into corruption. Taylor had barely escaped indictment. I would have surely been collateral damage. Our romantic relationship was irrevocably damaged. Our business relationship was uncertain.

It took me all morning to work up the nerve to call her. Tina's husband was washing the boat. I used his phone.

"It's Breeze," I said.

"Where are you?" asked Taylor.

"I'm here, in town," I told her. "What's up?"

"Not on the phone," she said. "Meet me for lunch?"

"If you're buying," I said.

"There's a new place at Fishville," she said. "Scotty's Brew House. Just opened."

"I'm on foot," I said. "It will take me twenty or thirty minutes to get there."

"Same old Breeze," she said. "When will you catch up to modern times? Maybe even get a phone."

"I'm just a simple man," I said. "I've made it this long."

"Start walking, boat bum," she said. "I'll meet you there in thirty."

Normally, I hated to be told what to do. I didn't take orders from anyone. Somehow, Taylor was different. She had the power to control the situation. I'd gotten right in line and agreed to do as she wished without even knowing I was doing it. Damn her. Part of the problem was my curiosity. Part of it was the desire to see her again. I'd sailed away from Holly for the second time. I had no prospects in the female companionship department. I liked being in the presence of pretty women. Taylor was as pretty as they came.

So I started walking. I took the Harbor Walk along the Peace River. I walked past the Tiki Bar and Hurricane Charley's. I hoped I wouldn't run into Cross-Eyed John in Gilchrest Park. I didn't have time for his shenanigans. I passed the tennis courts and the sailing club. I cut across the marina parking lot at Fisherman's Village. I found the new place. It was nice. So was the view when Taylor met me at the bar. She was wearing a tight dress that ended well above the knee. It accentuated her lovely figure. Matching high heels showed off her shapely legs. Her auburn hair framed her glasses and flowed around her face. She was a stunning apparition of feminine beauty.

I steeled my nerves. I tried to summon up the determination to resist her charms. I needed to maintain control of the conversation instead of letting her steer me. Instead, I blurted out "God, you're beautiful."

"Thank you, Breeze," she said. "You're looking pretty hot yourself. It's been too long."

"Pleasantries aside," I said. "Why am I here?"

"Let's get a drink first," she said. "Come on, have a seat."

She ordered white wine. I asked for a beer. We read our menus. The sexual tension was thick. That was the only good part of our past together. She hated my boat and lifestyle. I hated the world that she lived in. We were a terrible fit, except in the bedroom. I tried to keep a few things in mind. She was a cunning plotter, interested in advancing her own interests. She wanted to climb the political and social ladder. I was a tool to be used to further her ambitions.

"So what's this all about?" I asked.

"It's about Jimi," she said.

"What about him?" I asked.

"The fallout from his stunt continues," she said. "The whole affair is a thorn in my side."

"It's got nothing to do with me," I said.

"It's got everything to do with me," she said. "I'm on the hook for all of it. The victims are powerful people. They will stand between me and my goals, or worse, until this is resolved. I think you can help me resolve it."

"What makes you think I can help?" I asked.

"You know where he is," she said. "And you're very resourceful. You found him once already."

"I know where he was," I offered. "He's not there anymore."

"Where did you find him, Breeze?" she asked.

"Grand Cayman," I told her. "But like I said. He left."

"How do you know that?" she asked. There was nothing friendly in her tone. I was being cross-examined.

"I was there," I said. "I asked around for him. He's gone."

"Where is he now?" she demanded.

"I don't have a clue," I lied. "And I won't look for him for free."

"Do you think there's a reasonable chance of locating him?" she asked.

"I think it's worth a shot," I said. "What's the endgame? Are you looking to kill him?"

"These people want their money back," she said. "I have to get their money back. Do you understand?"

"What if I get the money back?" I asked. "How can I be sure they won't off him anyway?"

"I can't answer that," she said. "If they knew where he was, they might go after him."

"So I'll get their money without telling them where he is," I offered.

"How do figure on doing that?" she asked.

"Don't know yet," I admitted. "But I'll figure something out."

"That's my Breeze," she said, smiling. "Shit will just work out."

"I'm not your Breeze," I said. "Or anybody else's Breeze for that matter."

"There's not a woman in your life?" she asked.

"There was, and a damn fine one," I said. "But no, not now."

"What did you do to run this one off?" she asked.

"Long story," I said. "Deep matters of the soul and shit like that."

"Tell me all about it over dinner sometime," she said.

"I don't think so," I said. "Let's keep this professional."

"This will be my money," she said. "Not my clients. What's it going to cost me?"

"Fifty grand," I said. "Lots of travel expense."

"That's pretty steep," she said. "What if you find him but can't recover the money? How much just for his whereabouts?"

"I don't think I can give up his location," I said. "One of those goons is sure to kill him."

"I'll give you twenty-five just to tell me where he is," she offered.

"I'm not in the accessory to murder business," I said. "We do it my way or not at all."

"I'll give you half upfront," she said. "You'll get the rest after you get the money."

"I won't start until I see the upfront cash," I said.

"You at Laishley?" she asked.

"Yup, for a few days," I said.

"I'll bring it by the boat later," she said.

"Can you dress a little less sexy?" I asked. "We have a deal. You don't have to persuade me with your hotness."

"I thought that was what you were doing to me," she said. "I've never seen you looking so good."

"On that note," I said. "I'm gonna go. Catch you later."

"Goodbye, Breeze," she said. Even her voice was sexy.

I walked away the winner in that confrontation. She didn't know that I already knew where Jimi was. She didn't know that he was begging me to help him pay back the money. I'd help him. I'd collect fifty grand of Taylor's money doing it. Big win for Breeze. Easy money.

I went back to my boat and starting scraping varnish off the cabin top. I worked up a quick sweat in the Florida sun. The mindless work allowed me to think clearly. Was I missing something? Manipulating Taylor shouldn't have been so easy. She was sharp, and a seasoned liar. I was no dummy, but I didn't have her experience in the deceit department. Could she have played me somehow? I continued scraping and thinking.

What if she put a tail on me? What if I led her straight to Jimi? I'd have my twenty-five grand for finding him and giving up his location, just like she wanted. They'd beat the money out of him and kill him afterwards. He could offer to give up the money all he wanted, but he'd still be a dead man. This was something that Taylor would pull. If I find him, they find him. I couldn't let that happen.

The old paranoia returned. Was someone watching me already? I quit scraping varnish and grabbed a bottle of water. I casually looked around the marina. I moved aft to get a look at the park next door. I looked up at the bar above the marina. It was impossible to tell if someone was watching. I hadn't sensed anything wrong. Had my gut let me down?

Had I failed to pick up the signs? Maybe this mission wouldn't be as simple as I thought.

Maybe I was making up a danger that didn't exist, but I hadn't lived that long by taking unnecessary chances. I'd go forward as if someone was watching. I'd take precautions not to be followed, or to detect anyone that tried. The best way to do that was to untie the lines and take *Leap of Faith* away from land. Tough to tail a slow moving trawler without being seen. I didn't have a phone though. I needed to contact Jimi D. somehow.

I tried to work that out while I waited for Taylor. She showed up at six o'clock. She was wearing modest shorts and deck shoes. Her tank top fit loosely, showing a little bra strap now and then.

"Permission to come aboard, captain," she said.

"Granted," I said. "Thanks for wearing boat shoes."

"I didn't forget everything you taught me," she said. "I had to pull them out of the back of my closet and dust them off."

"Let's do this inside," I said.

"All business," she said. "You're not going to offer me a drink?"

"I've got beer and rum," I offered. "No wine."

"I'll take a beer if you're having one," she said.

There's not much room in the salon when the refrigerator door is open. We brushed hips as she made her way to her seat. She smelled heavenly. I handed her a beer and she patted the seat next to her, beckoning me to sit. I sat. She put her hand on the back on my neck and drew me to her. The kiss was long and deep. We parted long enough for her to pull her shirt off. Our lips stayed together while she fumbled at my shirt buttons. She stood and worked her shorts off. I took her hand in mine when she reached for my zipper. I held her at arm's length, just looking at her.

She stood in her bra and panties looking like a goddess of eternal love. Her body was without flaw. Her creamy skin was perfect. Her hair danced like a soft fire. A little angel spoke to me.

She's like heroin. You may enjoy the pleasure she provides, but she'll poison your soul.

I knew the angel was right. I tried hard to push her away. My arms wouldn't move. A little devil spoke to me next.

Look at her, dumbass! Do it. Take her now. She's so hot.

The devil had a point too. She was hot. Her fire would consume me. I found the will to say no.

"Stop," I said, separating myself from her. "We shouldn't do this."

"I know you want to," she said. "We are so good together."

"We were," I said. "I can't let you manipulate me."

"I'm not trying to," she claimed. "It's just sex. Have some fun, Breeze."

"You are one sweet temptation, girl," I said. "But I have to say no. Sorry."

"You really don't trust me, do you?" she asked.

"Not one drop," I said. "I wish I could. I really do."

"What can I do to earn your trust?" she asked.

She got down on her knees and pulled my zipper down. The snap was undone and my shorts were at my feet. Resistance was futile. All of my noble intentions went out the window. I didn't even curse my weakness. I just gave in to pleasure. Let my soul be poisoned, I thought. It was worth it.

We talked like old friends afterwards. She asked about the Bahamas. I told her some stories. We laughed and drank a few more beers. She had me good and loose when she started probing me for information on Jimi. How was I going to find him? Did I have any leads? How would I get the money? I snapped out of my post-blowjob daze and put a stop to it.

"I'll give you nothing until the job is done," I said. "Don't expect that to change. I find him. I get the money. You pay me the rest of what you owe me."

"What if you fail?" she asked. "He could be anywhere on Earth."

"Then you're out twenty five grand," I said. "But I won't fail."

"How can you be so sure?" she asked.

"I refuse to fail," I said. "Breeze always gets his man."

"Then he rides off into the sunset, alone," she said.

"Something like that," I said.

"You're incorrigible," she said.

"I just had the pleasure of a fantastically beautiful woman," I said. "And I'm twenty five thousand dollars richer. I must be doing something right."

"God, you're a frustrating man," she said.

"You need me to solve your little problem," I said. "Which I'll begin to do as soon as you leave."

"You kicking me out?" she asked.

"I think better when you're not around," I said. "You're very distracting."

"All right, I'll let you do your thing," she said. "I don't suppose you can keep me posted on your progress?"

"No phone, remember?" I said.

"You should really think about joining the modern world," she said.

"I'll take it under advisement, counselor," I replied.

She grabbed her purse and started for the door. She stopped short of opening it and turned back around.

"Don't let me down, Breeze," she said sternly.

It sounded like a threat.

Nine

I watched her walk up the ramp towards the parking lot. When she disappeared from sight, I followed. I wanted to see if she had anyone watching her, or me. She got in her car and drove off. Another car left just after she did. Maybe it was following her, maybe not. It could have just been coincidence. I made a quick scan of the area. Folks walked the Harbor Walk. Kids ate ice cream cones. Fishermen went back and forth from the tackle shop. It was a busy place. There was really no way to tell if someone was watching me. I decided to perform a little test.

I walked out of there towards the park. I was just a boater out for a casual walk, taking in the sights. As the sidewalk went under a bridge, I made a sudden U-turn and went back the way I'd came. A man in dress slacks and shoes hesitated as I approached him. He pulled himself together and continued walking. I was certain he was my tail. I watched him round the bend and sit on a park bench. I left the walkway and climbed up the hill. I sprinted across the highway to the other side of the bridge. I looked down at the man on the bench. He was looking around for me. Finally, he got up and walked back towards the marina.

He could stake out my boat easily enough, but they didn't have a beef with me. They just wanted me to lead them to Jimi. I decided to make a move before they could commandeer a boat to follow me. I went straight to *Leap of Faith* and fired up her engine. I threw off the lines and left the slip immediately. It was almost dark, but I didn't care. I knew Charlotte Harbor better than most. No boats followed me.

I made the turn at marker number five and watched the sun set over the Boca Grande Pass. It was very late when I made Pelican Bay. Taylor knew about this place. I wanted to see if they'd send a boat after me. Two days passed with no signs of surveillance. I pulled up anchor and headed back up the harbor. I didn't go to Punta Gorda.

Jimi was staying at Riviera. It was the worst excuse for a marina I'd ever seen. It was more of a junkyard, with decrepit docks and derelict boats. It was a good place to hide. I'd have to go up Alligator Creek to get there, so I anchored just outside the mouth of the creek. I just sat there all day, watching a few boats go by. None of them paid any attention to me. I spent the night in solitude. I detected no effort on the part of Taylor's partners to locate me by boat.

I took the dinghy up Alligator Creek to Jimi's hideout. I tied off to a bulkhead and walked towards the only decent looking sailboat in the place. The smell of cat urine permeated the air. The rats and the cats fought for dominance of this dump. It smelled like the cats were winning. I found Jimi sitting on his boat. He had a bandana wrapped around his face like a cowboy from an old western. I wasn't sure if it was to disguise himself, or guard against the stench. I startled him.

"Jesus, Breeze," he said. "You trying to give me a heart attack?"

"I take it this place doesn't see many visitors," I said.

"I told you," he said. "No one comes here."

"I've got good news and bad news," I said.

"Let's start with the good," he said.

"I talked to Taylor," I said. "She has hired me to get the money back."

"Hired you?" he asked.

"Yup, she's paying me to hunt you down and get the money out of you," I said.

"That's brilliant," he said.

"Now the bad news," I said.

"Uh oh," he said.

"I fairly certain they want you dead," I told him. "Even after you pay them back."

"What makes you think so?" he asked.

"Taylor tried to pay me just to locate you, for one," I said. "She may have had someone follow her to the marina, maybe not. I definitely picked up a tail the other day. So far they haven't followed my boat."

"So what's your advice?" he asked.

"Pay them back. Run and hide again," I offered.

"Will it ever blow over?" he asked.

"They won't search so hard if they get paid," I said. "But if they accidentally found you, they'd still take action. You can't hang around Charlotte County."

"Maybe I should have stayed hidden in the first place," he said.

"Too late for that now," I said. "There's Taylor to think about as well."

"I don't owe her anything," he said.

"She brought the clients to you," I countered. "You robbed them. I'd say you owe her big time."

"I guess you're right," he said. "I'll clear my conscience by getting this over with."

"How do you want to work it?" I asked. "Getting the money to them."

"I'll set up one offshore account in Taylor's name," he said. "You'll take her the account number and log-in information. She can distribute the cash to her cohorts."

"She'll probably agree to that," I said.

"Can you get her to agree not to come after me?" he asked. "I mean, I'm making things right here."

"It's not up to her," I said. "You burned those guys. They're the wild card here. I don't even know who they are."

"I know them," he said. "Enough to fear being caught by them."

"Set up the account," I said. "Give me what I need to take to Taylor."

"I need a few minutes," he said. "Make yourself comfortable while I fire up the laptop."

I listened to the click clack of his fingers on the keyboard. He muttered to himself at he transferred millions of dollars from a secret account into Taylor's new account. Tax avoidance at its finest. The IRS would never know about it. I figured Taylor was smart enough to keep it that way. When he was done, he went down below. He returned with a file folder.

"These are screenshots," he explained. "They show the exact amounts that I took from each account. It might prove useful to Taylor. These guys will try to rip her off."

"You held on to all that incriminating evidence?" I asked.

"I guess deep down, I always knew I'd be caught," he said. "I'm giving up before that happens."

"Let's hope they just accept repayment and leave you be," I said.

"Here's the account information, with username and password," he said. "Tell her to empty it as quickly as possible. I'll watch it. When the balance is zero, I'll erase all traces of it."

"Sounds like you've thought of everything," I said.

"Everything except how to live with the stink of cat piss," he said, laughing.

"This is a far cry from a penthouse suite on Grand Cayman," I said.

"That's why I need you to take me under your wing," he said. "Get me out of this dump."

"Keep laying low until the dust settles," I told him. "I'll be back. We can talk about it then."

"Thanks, Breeze," he said. "Really. I appreciate this."

I went back out to my boat with the file and account information. Jimi trusted me completely. I could simply use the infor-mation to make myself a multi-millionaire and disappear forever. I didn't even have a bank account though. Maybe Taylor was right.

Maybe I should join modern civilization, get a bank account and a phone. That thought lasted about three seconds. Screw that.

I spent another night anchored outside Alligator Creek. No one came looking for me. The sunset was spectacular. I went back to the marina the next day. As soon as I started walking up town, my tail from before followed. He didn't make any effort to conceal himself, just walked along behind me at a distance. When I made it to Taylor's office, he peeled off and disappeared.

I held my little package of million-dollar information tight to my chest.

"The fruits of my labors," I said to Taylor. "Which I'll gladly exchange for the rest of my pay."

"I'll need to look it over first," she said. "What have you got?"

"It's more like what you have," I said. "You're temporarily a very rich girl."

"I am?" she asked.

"Here's your account, with username and password," I said. "Here's what you need to properly distribute the funds. Jimi covered all the bases."

"Where is Jimi?" she asked.

"Not part of our deal," I reminded her. "I got the money. Now you have the money."

"I don't know why I keep underestimating you," she said. "How do you do it?"

"Trade secrets," I said.

"If you told me, you'd have to kill me?" she said.

"Something like that," I said.

"What's to keep me from running off with all these millions?" she asked. "Why didn't he return the money to each of them? He's got all the accounting right here."

"They didn't hire me," I said. "You did. What you do with it is up to you. But I'd advise prompt distribution."

"I'll take it under advisement, counselor," she said.

"I didn't let you down," I said. "Now don't let me down."

"Just a passing fantasy," she said. "But your righteousness is funny, coming from someone who so often lives outside the law."

"I know right from wrong," I said. "Regardless of my actions."

"No gray areas?" she asked.

"I missed that day in philosophy class," I said.

"Let's talk it over during dinner," she said. "We can celebrate your latest pay day."

"I'm not telling you where Jimi is," I said.

"You're infuriating, Meade Breeze," she said. "I had no such intentions."

"I'll just take my money and go," I said. "Maybe some other time."

"Are you afraid to be alone with me? She asked. "Afraid you'll give in to my charms?"

"You're a smart lady," I said. "My money, please."

She gave me a look of disapproval and went to a safe in the wall. She handed me a stack of bills, still in a bank wrapper.

"It's all there," she said. "I had confidence in you."

I didn't count it. I stuck in in my pocket and made my escape. I had to leave before I changed my mind about dinner, and what might happen afterward. I wasn't sure if I was being smart or stupid. No little angels appeared to advise me.

No one followed me back to the boat. Taylor must have called off the tail. I popped a beer and stared at the stack of money. Not bad for a few day's work. I fell into an easy payday. Jimi was begging to return the money anyway. The only loose end was whether they'd forgive and forget now that they'd been repaid. My business was done. I was in the clear on the whole affair. Jimi, on the other hand, was much less capable of living off the grid. He'd screw up sooner or later. If they found him, he'd be in deep shit.

I hung around the marina for a few more days. I didn't see anyone watching or following me. I paid my bill with Rusty and left. I anchored once again outside Alligator Creek. I waited another day just to be safe. I detected no surveillance. I went in to Jimi's junky marina and banged on his boat. He waved me inside.

"She's transferred all the money and I closed up the account," he said. "How did it go on your end?"

"I can't guarantee that you're off the hook, Jimi," I said. "Sorry."

"I've got to get out of this place," he said. "Help me. Teach me how to live like you do."

"It's not as easy as you think," I told him. "No showers, no clean laundry unless you wash it in a bucket. Bugs. Heat. You sure you don't want to go back to a condo in some exotic place?"

"My money wouldn't last long living like that," he said. "I learned that much."

"I'm not sure you're equipped to live on the hook," I said. "Generator? Solar panels? Water capacity? This boat is no real live-aboard."

"That's exactly what I need you to teach me," he said.

"We can't do it here," I said. "Too close to the heat."

"Where can we go?" he asked.

"Fort Myers Beach," I said. "I'll hide you in the backwater. I've got some friends there. We get you outfitted properly and then go from there."

"It's a start," he said. "When do we leave?"

"Tomorrow," I said. "Can you get out of the creek by yourself?"

"I brought her in here," he said.

"Just come out and follow me," I said. "We'll stop in Pelican Bay, so you know what that's all about. Then move south."

"I never anchored before," he said.

"Good grief," I said. "Show me your anchor locker."

We went forward to inspect the anchor, chain and rode. What he had was barely sufficient. He'd need a bigger anchor with more chain. I could see that his learning curve would be a long one. As we went through the critical parts of his boat, we saw someone walking towards us.

"Who is it?" I asked, hoping he knew.

"Dock master," he said.

The guy spoke to Jimi.

"Someone was at the gate asking about you," he said.

"Who was he?" asked Jimi.

"Didn't say," the dock master replied.

"What did he look like?" I asked.

"Dark hair, dress pants, dress shoes," he said. "Not a boater."

"Sounds familiar," I said to Jimi. "You gotta get out of here. Like right now."

"In the dark?" he said. "I don't know."

"The dude at the gate is the same dude that's been following me," I said. "I didn't lead him here by land. They're zeroing in on you somehow, though. We've got to go."

We got Jimi's motor running and lines untied. He followed my dinghy out of the creek and waited while I fired up *Miss Leap*. He followed me down the harbor to Pelican Bay. I didn't like his anchor or his anchoring technique, but the night was calm. He'd be okay. We began his education the following day. He didn't know much, but he was quick to learn. I fell into the role of teacher. He was a willing student. His life depended on it.

I explained how he shouldn't stay in one place too long unless he had concealment. I showed where he could get some cover there in the bay. He anchored way up behind the bar one night, and in the hurricane hole at the south end of Punta Blanca the next. We both pulled up and headed south for Fort Myers Beach.

He followed too closely. He used poor radio protocol. There was still a lot for him to learn.

Ten

Jimi's sailboat couldn't make it under the Sanibel Causeway on the Sanibel side. We had to go up the Caloosahatchee and through the Miserable Mile. I warned him three times about the side current that ran through that hazardous stretch. He still managed to run aground.

"I'm stuck, Breeze," he called over the radio.

"Pick a channel Jimi," I said. "And try to remember to hail by boat name, okay?"

"Channel 17?" he said.

"*Leap of Faith* to one seven," I replied.

"The *Whole Nine Yards* on seventeen," said Jimi. "He'd named his boat after a Bruce Willis, Mathew Perry movie.

"I warned you about that spot, dumbass," I said.

"What do I do know?" he asked.

"Did you get Sea Tow or Boat US?" I asked.

"Not yet," he admitted. "Just didn't get around to it. Didn't know I was leaving the dock so soon."

"Great," I said. "High tide isn't for another few hours."

"I'm supposed to just sit here and wait?" he asked. "Can't you pull me off?"

"I am not putting my boat at risk to save your dumb ass," I said.

"Come on, Breeze," he said. "I look stupid stuck here."

"That's because you are stupid," I said. "Listen, keep your engine running. Wait for a big power boat to come along, one that's throwing a big wake. Be ready to put it in gear when his wake lifts you up."

"That'll work?" he asked.

"If you get lucky," I said. "Some of those big yachts throw off a hell of a wake. If they slow down, call them on the radio. Ask them to purposely throw a wake at you."

"You gonna wait for me?" he asked. "I don't know where we're going."

"I'm going on through the bridge at Punta Rassa," I said. "I'll wait on the other side."

"Should I stay on channel seventeen?" he asked.

"No, go back to sixteen so you can call other boats and hear what's going on," I told him.

"I don't like this," he said.

"Then don't do it again," I scolded. "I won't be far. Call me when you get free."

I left him to ponder his mistake. He'd need to be more careful in these waters. Hopefully, he'd learn a lesson from it. On the Gulf side of the bridge, San Carlos Bay opened up. I could idle in place without being in the way of traffic. It wasn't long before a big cruiser came by throwing a four-foot wake. It rocked me pretty hard. It would rock Jimi too.

"*Leap of Faith* to *Whole Nine Yards*," I called.

"*Whole Nine Yards*," he came back.

"Go up one," I instructed.

"Up one," he answered.

"A big ass Carver is heading your way," I told him. "Nice big wake. Be ready to drive off that sandbar."

"I see him coming," he said. "Wish me luck."

"As soon as you feel some lift, drive off hard," I said. "Full throttle."

"Okay," he said. "Here we go."

A few minutes later I saw Jimi come under the bridge. I let him get close before turning for Fort Myers Beach. He followed close behind. There were dredges set up at the entrance to Matanzas Pass. I very sternly warned Jimi to steer clear of them. We hogged the middle of the channel just to be sure he wouldn't touch bottom again.

We steered around the mooring field and into the backwater where my friends lived. I dropped anchor five hundred yards north of Robin's boat. Jimi went to the south of Diver Dan's boat and threw his anchor out. One-legged Beth's boat was in the center of all of us. We made a motley collection of boat bums, although Jimi was too clean-cut and well-dressed to fit it properly. I made a mental note to advise him to grow a beard. A few months living back here would take care of his new sailing attire.

I put the dinghy in the water so I could make the rounds. I set up a meeting for later that day. No one turned down my happy hour invites. The party started at five. Diver Dan arrived with a big can of Foster's beer in his hand. Beth had once again sworn off alcohol. Robin had some weed, which I declined to share. To Jimi's credit, he didn't turn his nose up at my friends. Taylor had been horrified that I'd actually hang out with the lower class that these people represented. Dan used to dumpster dive. Beth had been homeless. Robin scraped by however he could. All of them had good hearts. They'd helped each other make a better life. They'd helped me from time to time. I'd made it possible for Dan and Robin to make some real cash, back when I was running coke. All of that was behind us now. They just wanted to be left alone to live as they chose.

If Jimi could be comfortable around them, it was a good omen for his ultimate future living this kind of lifestyle.

"Here's the deal," I told the group. "Jimi is hiding."

"What kind of trouble have you gotten into now?" asked Diver Dan.

"It's not my trouble this time," I said. "It's his. Some power people would like to find him."

"What did you do, Jimi?" asked Robin.

"I stole several million dollars," he said.

"What the hell you doing here, then?" asked Beth.

"With Breeze's help, I paid it all back," he said. "But I guess they're still mad."

"I knew you had something to do with it," said Dan. "You just can't stay away from trouble."

"Jimi tried to make things right," I said. "Give him credit for that. He may need your help."

"What can we do?" asked Robin.

"Let's all keep our eyes open," I said. "So far there is no indication that they have a boat, or want to get one to come looking for us, but let's be aware of strange boats snooping around back here. They know my boat. They don't know Jimi's."

"Them rental boats are through here all the time," said Dan. "How we supposed to know who's who?"

"The only guy I've seen, he's followed me twice and almost found Jimi, is about six feet tall," I began. "He's got short black hair, thinning on top. He was wearing long pants and dress shoes both times I spotted him. He's almost swarthy looking, not middle-eastern, but maybe Greek or Italian."

"A guy on a boat dressed like that would be easy to spot," said Robin. "Say he plays tourist and wears shorts and a tank top. What then?"

"I'd reckon he be white-legged for starters," I said. "I don't know, just keep a look out for anything suspicious back here."

"How do we get in touch?" asked Dan. "You get a phone yet?"

"Keep our radios on channel seventy-two," I said.

"Mine doesn't work," said Beth.

I gave her my spare handheld. Jimi gave them all his phone number. I asked Robin and Dan if they had weapons on board. Both replied in the affirmative.

"Let's hope it doesn't come to that," I said. "But keep them handy."

"I'm going to help out with this," said Dan. "But I want to suggest that you stop bringing this shit to our peaceful little piece of river."

"I hear you," I said. "Friends like you are in short supply. I didn't have anyone else to turn to."

"I appreciate that," he said. "Robin and I still owe you a favor or two I guess."

"No one owes anybody anything," I countered. "Just friends helping friends."

"I second that," said Robin. "We'll keep watch around here. Might be nothing anyway."

We had our perimeter set up, five set of eyes watching each passing vessel. I spent a lot of time on Jimi's boat, showing him how to read charts and going through his systems. We ran his sails up to inspect them and air them out. We changed his filters. I rewired the bilge pumps, replacing wire nuts with butt connectors and heat wrap. He asked a lot of questions. Mainly, he was concerned with how I spend my time. He was easily bored. He was going to have to get over that. I gave him some books to read. I told him that if he wanted to go to the beach, he would have to keep a low profile. I advised staying out of bars. If I was the guy looking for him, I'd check every bar on the beach first. It was how I'd found Jimi on Grand Cayman.

A week went by before anything happened. The silence of the afternoon was broken by Robin's voice on the radio.

"Bogey inside the wire," he said. "You hear me, Breeze?"

"I see him," said Dan. "He's coming downriver from Snook Bight."

"Keep your head down, Jimi," I said. "You copy?"

"I'm down below," he answered. "I can't see him."

"Stay down there," I said. "Saddle up boys,"

The mystery man who had followed me in Punta Gorda was driving a rented center console right towards *Leap of Faith*. I grabbed my shotgun and slid a round into the chamber. I had my finger on the safety when he pulled alongside.

"You try to board me, I'll smoke your ass," I told him.

Dan and Robin each appeared, guns leveled on the mystery man.

He put his hands up.

"You armed?" I asked him.

"Pistol," he replied. "Back of my waistband."

"You'll want to toss that overboard," I instructed. "Three guns to one remember. Don't try anything foolish."

"How'd you know I was coming?" he asked, plopping his gun over the side.

"This ain't my first rodeo," I said.

"Taylor warned me you were smart like that," he said.

"Taylor?" I asked.

"Shit," he said. "I shouldn't have let that slip."

"So Taylor sent you after me?" I asked.

"She thinks you'll lead her to Jimi," he said. "She wants him real bad. She said not to hurt you unless I had no choice."

"That's real sweet of her," I said. "But I don't know where Jimi is. Wouldn't tell her if I did."

"She's convinced you know," he said. "She thinks he's here, in Florida. Someplace close."

"What makes her think that?" I asked.

"We had eyes on you when you left the marina," he said. "We knew you spent a few days out near the coast. You stopped near Alligator Creek. You didn't really do anything or go anywhere. Next thing we know, Jimi has returned the money. You had to talk to him at one of those places. She said you got no phone."

"How did you find all this out?" I asked.

"Hired a local fishermen," he said. "Real old salty type. He's out there fishing every day. Said he knew your boat. Sees it all the time in Pelican Bay. Taylor knew to look there too."

"I'm flattered to have received so much attention," I said. "But it still won't help you find Jimi. He's long gone."

"I'll tell her you said so," he said.

"We won't ask questions if you come back here," I said. "We'll shoot first. You understand?"

"I'll be telling her where you are," he said. "And what you said about Jimi. No telling what she'll do with the information."

"Why does she still want Jimi?" I asked. "He's paid back the money."

"You'll have to ask her yourself," he said. "I just follow orders."

"Go on, beat it," I told him, with a wave of the shotgun. "Think long and hard before coming back here."

We all watched him drive away. No one spoke until he was out of sight. There'd been no sign of Beth or Jimi the whole time. The radio crackled.

"Is the coast clear?" asked Jimi.

"I'll be there in a minute," I said.

"I think you should leave here, Breeze," said Dan. "They send somebody out here when we're not around, might go badly."

"Agreed," I said. "We can't stay vigilant twenty-four seven."

"What about Jimi?" asked Robin.

"They don't know his boat, or even that he might be on one," I said. "That guy paid no attention to it just now."

"I think we'd feel better if he left too," said Dan.

"I'll talk to him about it," I said. "Thank you both for having my back."

"I'm too old for this shit," said Dan.

Dan and Robin hid their weapons and drove back to their boats. I was pushing it with them. It was too much to ask them to get involved in potential violence. The visit from mystery man flustered me. Why is Taylor pursuing me? I thought I had outsmarted her. I got her to pay me for something that took no effort on my part. I didn't give up Jimi's whereabouts. She even tried using sex to get it out of me. I thought I'd won. Now I was being watched and hunted. It didn't feel like a win anymore. I thought my running days were over.

This was Jimi's race to run. He was the problem, but why? He paid back the money. Why was Taylor still after him? There was more to the story than I'd be told. Not that there was anything honest about this whole affair, but someone hadn't been completely truthful. Either Taylor or Jimi had mislead me, or both. I could start with Jimi. He was waiting for me just up river.

Eleven

I went over to talk to Jimi. He didn't stick his head out until I was tied off.

"What happened?" he asked.

"Taylor's still looking for you," I said. "Any idea why?"

"How did they find you?" he asked. "I thought you were good at this stuff?"

"I'm in a slow boat," I said. "Taylor knows what it looks like and where I hang out. The only thing you have going for you now is that they don't necessarily know that you are on a boat, or what it looks like. I think we should part ways though. They'll come back to me, sooner or later."

"Where do I go?" he asked. "I don't know what I'm doing out here."

"We'll talk about it," I said. "First, you tell me why she's still after you."

"I screwed it all up, Breeze," he said. "I should have told you."

"What did you do, Jimi?" I asked.

"It was all her idea from the start," he said. "She set up the victims, sent them my way."

"She knew you were going to steal all the money right from the start?" I asked.

"Yes, she knew," he said. "We were supposed to split it."

"But instead you ran off to the Caymans," I said. "Why?"

"I figured out that I was the patsy," he said. "She'd feed me to the dogs and take all the money for herself. So I ran."

I let this new information sink in. Taylor had masterminded the plan all along. The money originally came from criminal activity. She used Jimi to hide it offshore. She'd get access from Jimi somehow, transfer it somewhere else, then she'd blow the whistle on Jimi. The bad guys would take him out, but they'd never get their money back. She'd have it hidden someplace else. It seemed like a dangerous game to play. I'd been right not to trust her, but I never imagined she'd go so far.

"Did she sleep with you, Jimi?" I asked.

"Yes," he said. "I couldn't help myself around her. She played me like a fiddle. I would have done anything she asked."

"She used her ample talents to try to get me to turn on you," I told him.

"And you resisted?" he asked.

"I didn't resist her talents," I said. "I just didn't give her what she wanted."

"God, she's hot," he said. "I've never been with such a gorgeous woman. She turned me to mush."

"We've got to figure out our next step," I told him.

"Run?" he said.

"I don't know yet," I admitted. "I'd like to turn the tables on her somehow. Get you free from this once and for all."

"How?" he asked.

"I'll figure something out," I said. "For now, let's get out of here."

Something dawned on me all of the sudden. If it was Taylor's plan to take the money for herself, why had Jimi transferred all of it directly to her? I asked him to explain it to me.

"I didn't just transfer the money," he said. "I transferred the responsibility."

"How so?" I asked.

"I emailed everyone involved, copying Taylor," he said. "I made a screenshot of the account I set up in her name. I told them the money had all been returned. See Taylor for repayment."

"What if she took off with it anyway?" I asked.

"Then they'd be looking for her, not me," he said.

"Good plan," I admitted. "Why do you figure she gave it up so quickly?"

"I'd say the heat was on her pretty good," he said. "She was responsible for the whole mess, after all. She sent them to me in the first place."

"She'll still want to find you," I said. "You double-crossed her."

"She ended up with nothing," he said.

"Plus, she's out the fifty grand she paid me to find you," I added.

"That was your double-cross," he said.

"Looks like we both outsmarted a very smart woman," I said. "She won't take it lightly."

"So let's just disappear," he said. "Take these boats and never be heard from again."

"I've had enough of running," I said. "There's got to be a way to expose her. Ruin her life."

"I feel lucky to have escaped her once," he said. "Why tempt fate? She might win the next one."

"We need a place to hole up," I said. "A base of operations. We'll come up with something eventually."

"Out of the way marina?" he asked.

"Good idea," I said. "I know a place off the beaten path. It's at Cape Haze."

"Cape Haze Marina?" he asked.

"No, the other one," I said. "Palm Island."

"That's pretty far from anything," he said.

"Precisely," I said. "Quiet and hidden away."

We made our vessels ready and headed north. I chose to run far out in the Gulf to avoid prying eyes on small boats. I even avoided the easy entrance to the inside route at the Boca

Grande Pass. Instead, I risked the notoriously tricky Stump Pass. I slowed way down and told Jimi to do the same. We creeped and crawled and picked our way inside without touching bottom even once. We turned back south for a mile or two until we reached Palm Island Marina.

I called the dock master on the radio and got our slip assignments. Dock hands were standing by to grab our lines and help us into our slips. After settling in, we met at the pool for a strategy session. Over cold beers, we tried to brainstorm a strategy to take Taylor down.

"With all this money bouncing around from here to Grand Cayman and back," I said. "Isn't there something illegal going on?"

"Believe or not," he said. "It's not illegal to transfer money to a safe offshore haven. They only thing illegal is how they made the money in the first place. Taylor has already beaten whatever charges they faced. So that's a dead end."

"What about the IRS?" I said. "Can't we blow the whistle on her?"

"She moved that money out real fast," he said. "Then I erased all traces of the account. I couldn't implicate myself."

"That bitch is a crooked as they come," I said. "There's got to be something we can do."

"Excuse my ignorance," he said. "But what else has she done that I don't know about."

"She bribes judges to win cases," I said. "That's how she kept me out of jail."

"How can we use that against her?" he said. "Without implicating you."

"Hell, Jimi," I said. "She went all the way to the Attorney General to stop an investigation. I helped her do it. She's connected with all the other crooks in both the judicial system and the government."

"It's tough to fight city hall," he said.

"What do you know about searching court records?" I asked.

"It's public information," he said. "What are we looking for?"

"I don't know exactly," I said. "What if we studied the cases of the people you stole from? Identified the judges. Developed some kind of pattern."

"She's a defense attorney," he said. "She defends people accused of crimes. It's all going to look sordid to us. But that's how the system works."

"What if we could figure out who she bribed?" I asked. "We get to them with a blackmail scheme. Force them to come clean."

"I don't know how to do that," he said. "I wouldn't know where to start."

"We could start with my judge," I said.

"Too risky," he answered. "All you know is that he took your bribe. You committed a crime too."

"Taylor is the one who gave him the money," I said. "I could claim ignorance."

"Her word against yours," he said. "Who do you think they'll believe? A respected officer of the court or an anonymous boat bum?"

"Good point," I admitted. "I appreciated her lawlessness when it worked to my benefit."

"You were blinded by her beauty just like I was," he said.

"I was more blinded by my desire to stay out of jail," I said. "But yea, another good point."

"So where does that leave us?" he asked.

"How do we get all the records of her cases?" I asked.

"For some things, you just have to ask," he said. "Freedom of Information Act. Other things you can go to the courthouse and search records. Civil cases I think."

"We need a lawyer on our side," I said.

"No lawyer is going to conduct a secret investigation into the conduct of another lawyer," he said. "It's unethical."

"Plenty of unethical lawyers," I said. "It's kind of a redundancy."

"What about a prosecutor that Taylor's beaten out of a guilty verdict?" Jimi asked.

"It's a start," I said. "We identify the prosecutors on our money guys. At least one of them has to be pissed off at Taylor."

"We study them a little bit," he said. "Try to see who might be approachable."

"Better than nothing," I said. "Did you leave a car at Cat Shit Key?"

"I did," he said. "How do we get it?"

"Make friends Jimi," I said. "Give away beers until you get someone to give you a ride."

"What are you going to do?" he asked.

"Write down the names of the guys we're looking into," I said. "I'll use your laptop. They have Wi-Fi here."

"I'd rather do that job," he said.

"Trust me, Jimi," I said. "You're much better at the people thing than I am."

I had a list of five names. There was no common denominator that tied these men together, except Taylor. Their criminal enterprises were diverse. They ranged from a billion dollar Ponzi scheme to selling contaminated Chinese drywall. One of them had ties to a New York crime family. One of them was a Medicare fraudster. One name raised a red flag. Thomas Fiore had been busted by an undercover agent who offered to provide access to foreign bank accounts in order to launder criminal cash. Taylor had gotten him off for that charge, plus charges of drug trafficking and the sale of stolen goods.

His case seemed like a good one to start with. Newspaper and internet articles lacked all the information that I needed. Who was the prosecutor? Who was the judge? I needed court records. I planned to let Jimi do that digging. I went back to the pool to find him handing out beers like candy on Halloween.

"Hey, Breeze," he said. "Meet my new friends, Matt and Bruce."

Matt and Bruce both lived on tiny sailboats. Bruce had an old Corvette. He wouldn't let anyone drive it, but he'd be happy to give one of us a ride. His car could only hold one passenger. Matt drove a beat up old Chevy truck. The bed was full of junk, as was the passenger seat.

"You guys want to make a few bucks?" I asked.

"What do you have in mind?" asked Bruce.

"Jimi left his car at his old marina," I said. "I'll give you each a hundred if you go pick it up for him."

"Why don't I just take Jimi to get it?" he asked.

"To be honest," I said. "Jimi is laying low. He shouldn't be seen picking up his car."

"I don't know man," said Matt. "Could it be dangerous?"

"No way," I said. "If someone is watching his old marina, they won't even know it's his car you're picking up. They don't even know what boat he's on. But they would recognize him if he showed up in the parking lot."

"What if they follow us?" he asked.

"If anyone is behind you on Placida Road, stop at Publix," I said. "If someone follows you out of there, stop at the post office. Don't turn in here if anyone is behind you at all. Go get a beer or something."

"A hundred bucks each?" asked Matt.

"Easy money," I said.

They took the money. Jimi gave them the keys. We'd have wheels in a few hours. I told Jimi what I'd learned so far. He poked around Google for a while and found out a little bit more. The original case had been transferred to Charlotte County from Dade County. The local prosecutor's office had been ill-prepared. Taylor had the hearings moved up and the entire case accelerated. The judge had given her all the leeway she wanted. The prosecutor got no such treatment. Half the charges were summarily dismissed. Fiore was found innocent on the remaining charges. It was a big win for Taylor, and an embarrassment for the prosecution. We needed to talk to him.

His name was Stephen Russell. He was now a State's Attorney. His loss in Fiore's case hadn't hurt his career. His office was in Fort Myers.

"Do you really think we can get somewhere with this?" asked Jimi.

"You have a better idea?" I asked. "Because I'm all ears."

"Maybe make a bunch of anonymous tips to all the right people," he said. "Cause a stir. Put Taylor back on the hot seat."

"Who was the judge on this case?" I asked.

"The Honorable Leigh F. Hayes," he answered. "A woman."

"Any information on her?" I asked.

"She's in Lee County now," he said. "Same building as our State's Attorney."

"Interesting that they both left Charlotte County after the Fiore trial," I said.

"Coincidence?" he asked.

"I never trust in coincidence," I told him. "That case was rigged from the start and they all knew it. Their cooperation was rewarded."

"There's no way you could know that for sure," he said.

"Educated guess," I said. "Call it speculation if you want, but that's what I think happened."

"What's that mean for us?" he asked.

"It means they probably won't cooperate with us," I said. "They won't welcome any renewed interest in the case."

"So we've got nothing," he said.

"We know more than we did yesterday," I said. "What can we do with our new information?"

"This stuff is giving me a headache," Jimi said. "Let's take a break."

We took more beer back to the pool and waited for Bruce and Matt. That part of the marina also had a hot tub, shaded pavilion with a refrigerator and microwave, and showers. The facilities were clean. There were no screaming kids to disturb the peace. Boats ran by on the ICW. There was a nice beach just across the waterway. I liked it there. Maybe I could come back and stay after we cleared up this mess.

In this past, whenever I found myself in a sticky situation, it was because I had found trouble. My own poor decisions had brought it on. This time, trouble had found me. Both Jimi and Taylor had sought me out, for different reasons. Why had I decided to help Jimi? Why didn't I just wash my hands of the whole affair? Jimi had stolen my money too. I'd tracked him down and gotten it back. He added a nice bonus in exchange for my promise not to give him up. I guess I still felt indebted to that promise. I hadn't given him up. Now that he'd repaid the stolen money, I was happy with that decision.

Learning that Taylor was evil had thrown a wrench into things. I'd really cared for her at one time. I thought we had a shot to make it as a couple. I thought we'd run away to some tropical paradise together. Her corruption sickened me now. Not that I was an angel, but she was clearly on another level of lawlessness all together. My crimes had been committed in order to survive. Her crimes were intended to thrust her into the spotlight and climb the ladder of success. I'd scraped and scratched in order to eat and put fuel in my boat. She'd clawed her way over the bodies of others to get to the top. She used her good looks to disarm you, before putting a knife in your back.

I wanted to make her pay. I wanted her to realize that she couldn't use people like Jimi to further her own agenda. She'd involved me in her deceit one too many times. I couldn't let it stand. I had to do something. She was playing a dangerous game. I often played dangerous games myself. I was good at it. I was determined to win this one.

I'm coming for you, Taylor.

Twelve

Jimi came to me with additional research on the other crooks Taylor had defended in court. Not every case, just the ones Jimi had stolen money from. It was tough to see how we could get any of them to cooperate with us.

Joel Steinger was the CEO of a private company, Mutual Benefits Corporation. He was the Ponzi scheme guy. He specialized in buying the life insurance policies of terminally ill patients for pennies on the dollar. He was politically connected to Senator Marco Rubio. It was widely believed that he helped a South American drug cartel launder money. He was too big of a fish for us to fry.

Carlos Beruff was the owner of Medallion Homes. He was the Chinese drywall guy. When new home buyers complained, he shut them up through intimidation. He seemed blue collar enough to approach at first, but he was running against Rubio for Florida's senate seat. Blackmail might work, we thought.

Stanley Phillips was also in construction. He was employed by Day and Zimmerman International as a foreman. He had used his position to direct contracts to shell companies that he owned. The work was done by his employer, but the money went to his fake cover companies.

Philip Esformes was the Medicare fraud guy. He opened up bogus clinics and made all sorts of fabricated claims. He'd gotten away with it for a long time. His current whereabouts were unknown.

Thomas Fiore had presumably returned to New York. He'd been recalled by the Bonanno crime family after his brush with the Florida legal system. Both the prosecutor and the judge in his case had moved on to bigger and better things.

Jimi wanted to find out how Taylor had gotten them off, but I didn't think it mattered. No amount of legal wrangling or technicalities could have allowed them to walk free. Taylor had paid off the right people, using her client's money. She'd directed them to Jimi as a way to separate them from large amounts of cash. She planned to rob them of their ill-gotten gains, sacrificing Jimi in the process. Two of them were huge power players in Florida politics. She had dirt on them. Maybe she saw a future for herself in politics. She'd make a great candidate. Several million dollars would jump start her war chest. She was dirty, but no more so then the rest of them.

I was out of my league. These people lived in a different universe than I did. I didn't see a way to use any of them to my advantage. I didn't know how I'd ever even gain an audience with them, if I did figure out a plan of attack. I expressed my frustration to Jimi. We were partners in this thing. I couldn't do it all myself. He thought it over. I saw the light come on in his eyes when he hit on something.

"We've got to put you in their world," he said. "Make you one of them."

"I'm not following," I admitted.

"We create a new identity," he said. "Give you a reason to talk to them. Make you a power player too."

"Me?" I asked. "Look at me, Jimi. I am, and always will be, a boat bum."

"We can change that temporarily," he said. "Get you a fancy suit and cut your hair. Fake business cards, fake title, make you someone important."

"I'm skeptical," I said. "Important how?"

"A Political Action Committee," he said. "Consultant or whatever."

"That might work with Beruff," I said. "Maybe even the State's Attorney."

"What angle would you use?" he asked.

"I'm looking to make a donation and bring to bear considerable political influence," I said. "But my people are worried about that case Taylor handled for him. Wouldn't want any illegalities exposed at his point."

"I like it," he said. "You sound like a political hack already."

"I don't look like one," I reminded him.

"I can fix that," he said. "Let's order business cards. While we wait for them to be printed, we'll give you a makeover."

"What's my PAC named?" I asked.

"I don't know," he said. "You can think up something."

"Am I a Democrat or Republican?" I asked. "I haven't kept up on politics at all."

"Let's go with Independent," he said. "We can pretend to throw money to both sides, if necessary."

"Independent Florida," I said. "Super PAC concerned with Florida issues."

"I'll file some paperwork," he said. "In case anyone checks, you'll have a seemingly legit organization."

"I'll call myself Winston Shade," I said.

"Perfect," said Jimi. "How'd you come up with that?"

"It was the name of my stock broker back in the day," I said. "I always thought it was a cool name."

"Winston Shade," he said. "Political Consultant. Point man for Independent Florida."

Over the next few weeks, Jimi helped me transform myself into Winston Shade. He took me to a salon in Venice. I got a fancy haircut and a manicure. I tried to balk at the manicure, but he assured me that all the powerful people had them. It was part of the image. We drove all the way to West Palm Beach. He picked out an Armani suit for me. The tailor promised to have it ready in a few days. I got five hundred dollar shoes and a Rolex watch. He made me stop wearing sunglasses. He said I needed to get rid of my raccoon eyes. I laid by the pool with my eyes closed for a week to put a tan on the white areas left by constant sunglass wearing.

Jimi admonished me for poor posture.

"Head up, shoulders back," he kept telling me. "Walk with a purpose. Show them you belong."

We sent out fake press releases for Independent Florida. Our PAC was deeply concerned with the environment in south Florida. We were against the status quo. We demanded real change. We did not endorse candidates. Instead, we encouraged voters to turn against incumbents. Jimi created a website. We made some videos of blue-green algae on both coasts. We blasted Senator Bill Nelson for taking so much money from Big Sugar. We called on Governor Rick Scott to send the water south into the Everglades.

Jimi worked tirelessly to put the name Independent Florida on the map. I worked on my tan. The internet was a wonderful thing. I never realized it's potential. I didn't even own a phone. In a short time, two guys on a boat with a single laptop, had created a movement. Soon we were contacted by various environmental groups. I met with their leaders, spreading my new business cards everywhere. I made some small donations to their causes. Thanks to Jimi's internet wizardry, Winston Shade appeared to be everywhere. One day he didn't exist. The next day he was major player.

We started sending out feelers to Carlos Beruff's people. He needed money. It looked like we had some. Eventually, he asked for a meeting. I agreed, with certain conditions. It had to be private. No cameras, no news clips. Jimi rented a Lexus for me to show up in. I was nervous, but I kept my head up and my shoulders back. I walked in like I belonged there.

"Thanks for meeting with me, Mr. Shade," said Carlos. "But I'm not certain what we are here to discuss."

"Winston is fine," I said. "I'm here to get acquainted. Maybe discuss your political future. Independent Florida has been watching your race with keen interest."

"I never heard of you people until yesterday," he said. "What kind of influence can you have?"

"Our PAC is simply a clearing house for wealthy donors who wish to remain anonymous," I told him. "So far, they are on the sidelines. I can change that."

"Am I supposed to try to win your endorsement," he asked. "Or can I expect a significant donation?"

"Not so fast," I said. "There's one small matter we'd like to clear up."

"What's that?" he asked.

I cleared my throat and leaned in closer. I spoke softly, as if I didn't want anyone else to hear.

"Taylor Ford," I said. "I believe she represented you in an alleged criminal matter?"

"What about her?" he asked.

"We believe she bought your innocence," I said.

"Preposterous," he snorted. "I was innocent. The judge agreed."

"Our group has acquired some inside knowledge of your case," I said. "We are fairly certain that Miss Ford bribed the judge. The prosecutor looked the other way. He was rewarded too."

"How could you or anyone else know about any of this?" he asked. "Why are you really here?"

"This indiscretion does not disqualify you from receiving our support," I said. "We just need to come to an understanding."

"Understanding of what?" he said. "I won't be bought Mr. Shade."

"All political contributions come with expectations, Mr. Beruff," I said.

"What do you want from me?" he asked.

"We may decide to make a move against Miss Ford," I said. "Expose her. Have her disbarred, maybe even sent to prison."

"I can't help you without exposing myself," he said.

"So you were aware that she did indeed bribe the judge?" I asked.

"Let's cut to the chase, shall we?" he said.

"In exchange for a large contribution, you'll cooperate," I said. "We help make you the next senator from Florida. You help us take out Taylor Ford."

"How?"

"We'll insist on your innocence," I said. "But we'll need a statement. She tried to get you to agree to bribe the judge, but you refused."

"I'd really rather not get involved in this right now," he said. "Poor timing."

"You won't be the focus," I told him. "We'll have another case to nail her with, but you're in the news these days. Your statement will go a long way to incriminate her. It was also bolster your credentials as a law and order candidate."

"How much we talking?" he asked.

"What's it going to take?" I asked back.

He named a figure. I told him I'd consult with the donors and get back to him. We shook hands and I left. I was amazed at how little it took to buy a politician. Winston Shade had worked his first big political con job. I was one step closer to burning Taylor.

Back at the marina, I continued to carry my new persona. I got out of the Lexus and walked straight and tall to the pool. Jimi was beside himself.

"Man, you look like James Bond," he said. "The Pierce Brosnan one. How'd it go?"

"He rose to the bait," I said. "He all but admitted his guilt and the bribe. He's willing to play ball for a price."

"How do you do it?" he asked.

"Do what?"

"You just walked in and pulled the wool over a politician's eyes," he said. "I'd be scared shitless."

"I just try to stay cool," I said. "I keep my cool and roll with it. Shit works out."

"You're something else," he said. "When I first met you, I thought you were nothing more than the boat bum you portray."

"I am a boat bum," I said. "No fancy haircut or manicure is going to change that."

"You've got some weird skills," he said. "Like how you found me down in the Caymans. Like how you've left a trail of beautiful women behind you. Like how you outsmart both criminals and politicians. It's unnatural."

"Just lucky, I guess," I said. "Don't go getting all gay on me, Jimi. Not that there's anything wrong with that."

We both laughed and opened a new beer. I did look pretty good in my new duds. If only Taylor could have seen me in action. I wasn't ready for that yet. Winston Shade had more work to do. On Jimi's advice, I changed out of the fancy clothes so I wouldn't get them dirty. He hung them properly and covered them up with plastic. I changed into shorts and a fishing shirt. I put a hat over my expensive haircut. We went to his boat to plot our next move.

Thirteen

I had my eye on that state's attorney down in Fort Myers, but first I needed to pad Winston Shade's resume. I started making appearances at various protests held by citizen's groups. I didn't chant or try to get myself on TV. I stood by quietly, and met with the leaders afterwards. I made myself known to as many groups as I could find. Southwest Florida Citizens for Clean Water, Captains for Clean Water, The Everglades Foundation and others, all welcomed me as a new supporter. The environment was a hot topic in south Florida so I rolled with it.

I made Independent Florida synonymous with the clean water movement. I kept spreading those business cards around. Eventually, I called all the groups together for a meeting. I wrote them all checks from the Independent Florida account and promised to promote their cause in political circles. I signed the Now or Neverglades petition. I made vague statements about having the support of wealthy people. The mysterious anonymous donors I referenced had more influence than if they were real. Everyone wanted money from me. Money that I didn't really have. What I had was an air of authority. Winston Shade looked like a man who got things done. I kept my head high and my chest out. I kept my shoes shined and my rented Lexus clean. No one could tell that I didn't even have a driver's license.

Winston Shade was gaining enough notoriety, it was a matter of time before he and Taylor crossed paths. I decided it was time to move on the state's attorney. My assistant, Jimi, asked for an appointment with Stephen Russell. Mr. Russell was happy to meet with Mr. Shade.

His desk was flanked by the Florida state flag and the American flag. His thick round rug was a replica of the state seal. His shelves held law books. His degrees hung on the wall behind him. He was a stout man, with wide shoulders and a thick neck. Even his brown hair was thick. He wore thin gold-framed glasses over his thick nose. He wore a sensible brown suit. His crisply knotted tie was a lighter shade of brown. I stood in my Armani suit and expensive shoes, looking at my Rolex, until he recognized my presence.

He stood and motioned for me to sit. He didn't offer to shake hands.

"State your business, Mr. Shade," he said. "I don't generally entertain political consultants."

"Because your job is not a political one," I said "It's all about the law and its above politics, right?"

"That's correct," he said. "So why are you here?"

"That's bullshit," I said. "It's always about politics. You know it and I know it. Everything is political in south Florida."

"What do you want from me, Mr. Shade?" he said. "Is there something I can help you with?"

"There's something I can help you with," I said.

"How can you help me?" he asked.

"I can help you with your political ambitions," I said. "Whatever they might be. I can guarantee you a seat in the state house. I might even be able to get you to Washington."

"What makes you think I have an interest in politics?" he asked.

"Look, you were a prosecutor forever. Now you're the top man in five counties," I said. "Outside of Miami, you're the most powerful lawyer down here. It's only natural that you'd seek public office."

"And you can help me with that?" he asked. "What do you want from me? Clean water, save the Everglades stuff?"

"Naturally," I said. "But's there another little matter that is of greater interest to me."

"What's that?" he asked. "I'm not sure I like where this conversation is going. If you're acting as a lobbyist, there may be some impropriety."

"I appreciate your desire to maintain the letter of the law," I said. "This is more of a personal matter. One that you are uniquely qualified to understand."

"I'm not following," he said. "Just get down to your point."

I think he was interested in running for office, but he was totally no-nonsense. He wasn't sure what I was trying to accomplish, and he didn't like being in the dark. He was a man used to controlling things. He'd take my money, but only if it was a legal transaction. I'd thrown him with the mention of a personal matter.

"I'm interested in a certain attorney," I said.

"I'm the chief attorney," he said. "I should know them all."

"Taylor Ford," I said, watching his eyes.

I saw what I was looking for. He clenched his teeth ever so slightly at the mention of her name. He looked down for a brief second. He brought his gaze back to mine.

"What is your interest, exactly?" he asked. "And why do you think I can help?"

"The Thomas Fiore case," I said.

"Are you an attorney, Mr. Shade?" he asked. "I have no obligation to discuss an old case with you."

"Did you know what was going down?" I asked. "Or were you an innocent bystander?"

"I don't know what you're talking about," he claimed.

"Yes, you do," I said. "He should have never been found innocent. You were the prosecutor. Did you fail miserably or was the fix in?"

"Why should you care about Thomas Fiore?" he asked.

"I don't give a shit about him," I said. "I'm here to advance a political career, but I can't in good conscience support you for dog catcher if you took a bribe."

"I did not take a bribe," he said. "I can assure you of that."

"It was the judge then?" I asked.

"Leigh Hayes," he said. "They got to her somehow."

"And you just stood by," I said. "You didn't even get paid to participate in a travesty of justice."

"It wasn't like that at all," he said.

"How did they get you to go along then?" I asked.

"It was the carrot or the stick," he said. "I could die in the local prosecutor's office, or I could take this job."

"And Taylor was behind all of it?" I asked.

"I never knew for sure," he said. "She was the bag man. She paid Hayes. Fiore was her client."

"Are you aware of other instances like the Fiore case?" I asked.

"Rumors mostly," he said. "Folks said Taylor had important friends."

"I want to take her out," I said. "I want you to help."

"In exchange you'll back me in a run for office?" he asked.

"That's what I'm offering," I said. "But she has to fall."

"How do I know you carry any weight, Mr. Shade?" he asked. "You seem to have burst on the scene rather quickly."

"Folks say I have important friends," I said.

"Then you won't mind if I check into you before I make up my mind?" he asked.

"You can check into Independent Florida all you want," I said. "But you won't find Winston Shade."

"Why not?" he asked.

"Not my real name," I said.

I dropped my business card on his desk and walked out. I kept my head high and my chest out.

Back at the marina, I instructed Jimi to make sure that Independent Florida would withstand scrutiny. He set to work on our legal filings, making sure all the requirements were met and looked legitimate. We transferred more funds into the PAC's bank account. I asked him to stand by to answer phone calls and emails. Winston Shade needed a break.

Rubbing elbows with members of the legal profession and aspiring politicians, while pretending to be someone I was not, had caused me some anxiety. I had maintained my cool throughout, but I was afraid I couldn't keep up the façade forever. Someone would figure out my scam. Winston Shade would pop up on Taylor's radar eventually. What was I going to do then?

I decided to disappear for a while. I'd let Beruff and Russell stew things over while I took a vacation. I hoped their ambition would lead them to cooperate. In Russell's case, I had also appealed to his sense of justice. I had a feeling he'd be willing to work with me. He felt resentment towards Taylor. Beruff was a wild card. He was trailing Rubio badly in the polls, barely garnering ten percent support among Republican voters. Rubio didn't even mention him, instead focusing his attention on his Democratic opponent.

I wanted to take my boat someplace quiet. I wanted to just sit still and relax for a few days. Normally, that would mean a trip to Pelican Bay, but Taylor's people might decide to pay me a visit. I didn't want to get too far away. I needed a new place to hide out. That fisherman who'd pointed me out for Taylor's goon was a problem. If he was out in the harbor every day, he'd see me no matter where I went. I sat down with my chart book and got creative. I didn't need amenities. I could even do without a beach for a few days. I just wanted some peace and quiet. I wanted a place where no one would spot me, even accidentally. I decided on a lake off the Myakka River. I'd been up there a few times to haul out the boat for new bottom paint. Everyone used one of the yards near Placida for bottom jobs. I'd have to navigate the lock with no help, but I could manage it. I'd anchor in the wide open area before approaching the boat yards. It was about as isolated as one could get near Charlotte Harbor.

I forgot to stock up on bug spray. I made it through the first night, but exhausted what little spray I had. The second night was brutal. I had no choice but to close up and sit inside. It was unbearably hot. I got no productive thinking done. I sat in my own sweat, swatting mosquitoes. A breeze blew up nicely on day three. I could sit out on the back deck without being eaten alive. Boat traffic had been nonexistent until then.

I saw a familiar looking sailboat enter the lake, heading towards the boat yards. No doubt about it, it was *Another Adventure*. I couldn't believe it. I couldn't stop smiling either. I hailed Holly on the radio.

"Damn, Breeze," she said. "Are you even allowed to anchor there? Of all the bodies of water in all of Florida, I find you again."

"You headed up to haul out?" I asked.

"I have an appointment tomorrow," she said.

"Drop the hook here," I said. "Let's catch up."

"It's great to see you, Breeze," she said. "We've got a lot to catch up on."

She appeared to be alone. I saw no crew, not even Tim. I watched her drop anchor. She got settled on the hook and threw a kayak over the side. She paddled over alone.

"What happened to your boyfriend?" I asked.

"He decided to go spastic on me after too much liquor," she said. "Started punching holes in shit and throwing my stuff overboard. I lost two wet suits. Lost him too."

"I'm sorry to hear that," I said, not quite honestly. "He seemed like a good kid."

"He is a good kid," she said. "Just can't behave when he's drinking."

"Speaking of drinking," I said. "You want a beer?"

"Believe it or not," she said. "I've been dry since that night."

"Good for you," I said, again not quite honestly. "Mind if I have one?"

"Knock yourself out," she said. "You never had a problem that I saw."

"When I drink beer, I get happy," I said. "When I drink rum, I go to sleep."

"What the hell are you doing up here?" she asked.

"Long story," I replied. "Just hiding out for a few days."

"What have you gotten yourself into now?" she asked.

"A very long story," I said. "But I did find Rabble."

"How'd it go?" she asked.

"He damn near killed me with a spear gun," I said. "But I got the money and left him tied up in the Everglades."

"Jesus," she said. "He'll be gator bait."

"I left him his machete," I told her. "He shouldn't have had any trouble getting free."

"You're not hiding from him are you?" she asked.

"He's the least of my worries," I said. "You remember the name Jimi D. don't you?"

"The guy who stole all the money," she said. "You called him to help that guy we tracked down in the Bahamas."

"Exactly," I said. "I've helped him pay back the rest money he stole. A certain person would like to see him dead anyway."

"Who?" she asked.

"Taylor," I said.

"Get out!" she yelled. "You're ex-girlfriend is trying to kill Jimi? Unreal."

"I've been helping him stay under the radar," I said. "He bought a boat."

"Where is he?" she asked.

"A quiet little marina just up the ICW," I said. "I have a slip there too."

"That's just a few miles from the boat yard," she said.

"Which one you using?" I asked.

"Safe Cove," she said. "Charlotte Harbor Boat Storage is full."

"I'll pick you up tomorrow before they lock the gate," I said. "Wear your best outfit."

"You have a car?" she asked. "Wonders never cease."

"Jimi has a car," I said. "Right now I have a rental."

"Where are we going?" she asked.

"Dinner some place nice," I said.

"A date?" she asked.

"Don't have to call it that, if you don't want to," I said.

"A date is fine," she said.

"Then it's a date," I said. "See you about five."

She went back to *Another Adventure*. I sat and pondered the odds. I hadn't wanted to be found. The one person who I'd be happy to see, had found me anyway. I took it as a good omen.

Fourteen

I went back to Palm Island Marina the next day. It was a tight place to get in to. I had to make a six-point turn before the boat was straight enough to slide between the pilings. Matt and Bruce were there to grab my lines. Jimi waved from the deck of *Whole Nine Yards*. After I got *Leap of Faith* tucked in, I went over to see Jimi.

"You're not going to believe it," he said.

"Believe what?" I asked.

"We're getting donations," he said. "I mean Independent Florida is getting donations."

"People are sending us money?" I asked.

"I put a donate button on the website," he said. "Plus I've gotten several calls and emails from potential donors."

"Big donors?" I asked.

"Sierra Club, Coastal Conservation Association, and private individuals who wish to remain anonymous," he said.

"My mystery backers," I said.

"They haven't given a cent yet," he said. "They want to see what direction the PAC will take next. They'd like to meet Winston Shade."

"What direction are we taking?" I asked.

"We stick with water quality, of course," he said. "But we add rooting out corruption."

"Brilliant," I said. "That should help us with the State's Attorney."

"Save the environment and get rid of crooked politicians," he said.

"And Lawyers," I added.

While I was gone, Jimi had bought me another suit. He used the original one to give the tailor guidance. He leased the Lexus for another six months. He gave me a list of emails to return and appointments to make. Winston was going to be a busy man, rooting out corruption and saving the environment. I combed through it all before telling Jimi that further action on my part was going to have to wait another day.

"Hot date," I told him. "Just down the street at Safe Cove."

"Only you could hide out in the wilderness and come back with a date," he said. "Who is she?"

"It's the cute Rasta chick from my Bahamian adventure," I said. "Holly."

"She just happened to appear out of thin air?" he asked.

"I anchored up inside the lock at Cattle Dock Point," I said. "She was on her way to the boat yard."

"Kismet," he said.

"Serendipity," I said.

"Fortuitous," he replied.

"Yea," I said. "Lucky."

I suited up before going to meet Holly. I combed my fancy haircut. I dusted off my expensive shoes. The suit had been freshly dry-cleaned. I even shaved for the occasion. I drove slowly into the boat yard. I didn't want to kick up dust and get the car dirty. I circled around until I saw *Another Adventure* up on blocks. Holly was sitting in the shade. She wore a flowery sun dress and flat white sandals. She didn't know who I was when I pulled up.

I got out of the car and walked towards her. I used my Winston Shade walk.

"Wow," she said. "Who the hell are you? And what did you do with Breeze?"

"The name's Shade," I said. "Winston Shade."

"What's this all about?" she asked. "You look stunning."

"As do you," I offered. "I'll tell you over dinner."

We went to a place called Zydeco Grille. It specialized in Cajun and Creole style meals. She ordered Jambalaya and I got the Etouffee with shrimp. I drank some fancy beer called Alita. Holly had ice water.

"This is exciting," she said. "But why do I sense there's a world of trouble behind your new look?"

"I know you'll find this hard to believe," I began. "But Winston Shade has been hanging out with politicians, State's Attorneys, and leaders of various political movements. He's become a real player in south Florida."

"Why?" she asked. "This just isn't you at all."

"That's the reason for the new identity," I said. "Breeze doesn't belong in the circles I've been running in."

"What are you trying to accomplish?" she asked.

"It's all to take down Taylor," I said.

"You've got an endgame?" she asked. "This is all going to work out according to a plan right?"

"Not exactly," I admitted. "I'm sort of winging it."

"Like you always do," she said. "You've changed, but you're still the same."

"I've made a lot of progress in a very short time," I said. "It will work out."

"Meanwhile," she said. "I'm on the hard for at least a week."

"You're more than welcome to stay with me," I offered.

"Are you speaking as Winston, or Breeze?"

"Whichever you prefer," I said.

"Let's stick with Winston tonight," she said, laughing. "He's sweeping me off my feet."

Back aboard *Leap of Faith,* Winston showed Holly a very good time. We joked about her sleeping with a stranger. In the morning, Breeze was back. I had on tattered shorts and ball cap. My flip flops were worn out. I had black under my fingernails from changing the oil in the generator. I had black on my nose from scratching an itch with oily fingers.

"That's my boy," said Holly.

"Good morning," I said. "When you're ready, I'll show you the showers. God knows I need one."

"Coffee first," she said.

We got cleaned up after breakfast and went to see Jimi. His lap top was on. He was talking on the phone. We waited for him to finish.

"You're in demand," he said. "I've set up two potential donor meets, and you got a call from the State's Attorney."

"Things are happening," I said.

"You also need to start throwing some of that money around," he said. "We can't keep honest donations."

"If Russell is onboard with the environmental stuff," I said. "We'll start his campaign fund for him."

"Okay, that's legit," he said. "I'll work on other avenues."

"Start making our anti-corruption stance public," I suggested.

"Gotcha," he said.

Jimi D. had created Facebook pages, Twitter feeds, Google+ accounts and blogs to support Independent Florida. Anyone perusing social media would think that our PAC was a big driving force staffed by dozens. Jimi spent at least twelve hours a day to further that perception. I didn't want him wandering out in public. There wasn't a whole lot to do otherwise, except sit in the pool or at the bar.

Holly and I both created a host of fake profiles. We used them to "Like" Jimi's posts and make comments, driving further discussion. We cross posted on all the water activist pages whenever it was relevant. Independent Florida's new emphasis on corruption was received favorably. Many of the people concerned about the Lake O discharges blamed the problem on corruption. Big Sugar was the main culprit. Bullsugar.org was formed to educate the public on the vast amounts of money they gave to politicians. Governor Rick Scott took a constant pounding on social medial, as did Senator Marco Rubio. The Water Management Board had been stuffed with Scott cronies. Carlos Beruff was even a member for a short time. Spots on the board for environmental concerns and the general public were vacant.

We tried hard not be partisan in our efforts, but Republicans ruled the roost in Florida politics. Rubio's counterpart in the Senate, democrat Bill Nelson, took tons of cash from Big Sugar as well. It was impossible to find a Florida politician who hadn't. Just as we were combining our water quality message with our corruption theme, the Water Management Board voted to allow even higher levels of toxins into the state's waters, specifically certain chemicals associated with fracking. I was a foreigner to these affairs. I barely knew what fracking was. I only knew that the waters of the Caloosahatchee River and Fort Myers Beach had been ruined. I'd seen the effects as far north as Captiva. Even the waters of Pelican Bay were darker and less full of life.

Jimi brought me up to speed. He pointed me to dozens of articles and blog posts on the topic. The more I read, the madder I got. Political corruption had sacrificed the health of Florida's ecosystem. It went back decades of course. Both parties had taken their turn running things. Both parties had turned a blind eye to pollution. Both parties were corrupt. Two of the biggest players in the sugar industry were the Fanjul Brothers. One of them donated heavily to Republican politicians. The other gave his blood money almost exclusively to Democrats. Their company, Florida Crystals, was more commonly known as Domino's Sugar. They were only half of the equation.

The Mott family ran US Sugar. They were responsible for skewing water management practices to protect their sugar production, rather than the fragile environment surrounding their growing operation.

Together they were referred to as "Big Sugar." They spent millions annually to influence not only local water control, but national subsidies for their product. Politicians at every level, regardless of party affiliation, had been eager to accept their cash.

We used this line of attack to endear ourselves to the activist community. Very quickly and subtly, we veered into the corruption of the legal system. I wanted to make the public aware of the criminal actions of people like Taylor and Judge Hayes. I wanted to tie corrupt businessmen, with corrupt lawyers and corrupt judges. People like the men Jimi had robbed, had been simply buying whatever piece of the system they needed to continue their illegal practices. It was all a vicious cycle.

We didn't quit on the environmental issues, we simply expanded our reach. This brought us new followers on social media, and new contributors. We had thousands of Facebook followers and a very active page. Jimi had been a wizard at drawing attention to Independent Florida. I'd used some of my own money to advertise on the PAC's behalf. Winston Shade was the face of Independent Florida. He was often quoted in news articles or referred to during water quality discussions. WINK News in Fort Myers referred to him as "a tireless fighter for clean water in Southwest Florida." It was better than holding a sign atop a bridge.

Still, it was all just idle talk. We'd help bring awareness, but the political will for a long lasting solution wasn't there. We couldn't compete with Big Sugar, or the entrenched corruption that fed off of it. My real target was Taylor. We'd made Winston Shade appear important. I had the ear of the State's Attorney. I'd gotten an audience with Beruff. Who knew where it could lead?

I put on the newer suit for my appointment with Stephen Russell. Holly messed with my new hairdo until she was satisfied. She laughed at my GQ look, as she called it. She much preferred the real Breeze. I drove to Fort Myers feeling confident.

Russell was more welcoming this time. He shook hands and offered me a seat. He almost smiled.

"You've been a busy man since we last talked," he said. "You're everywhere."

"That's my staff," I told him. "I've got great people who are dedicated to real change."

"They are doing a great job getting the word out," he said. "I've been watching."

"I assume you found our PAC a legitimate entity?" I asked.

"By all appearances," he said. "And nothing on Winston Shade, just like you said. Why is that?"

"I'm just an actor," I said. "I don't have any power or money. I'm just the mascot."

"The real power and money is behind the scenes," he said.

"Such as it is," I said. "I can't divulge much about that."

"I'd like to know that I'm not throwing in with mobsters," he said.

"Not that I'm aware," I said. "Everyone supporting our efforts truly cares about the issues we've spoken to."

"That's reassuring," he said. "I care about the same issues. I'd like to further explore your support for my run for office."

"I've sworn to use our donor's money to further our clean water crusade," I said. "That's imperative."

"I'm onboard with that," he said.

"And I personally want to ruin Taylor Ford," I said. "Do you understand?"

"That's where it gets tricky," he said.

"Is this an integrity thing?" I asked.

"I could move against her while still maintaining my integrity," he said. "It's the system you're up against."

"A corrupt system," I said. "You're at the top of it. Real integrity would move you to solve the problem."

"I don't blame you for thinking that way," he said. "But you don't realize what you're asking."

"Asking the State's Attorney to root out corruption within his district doesn't seem that unreasonable," I said.

He got up from his chair and paced around the office. He stopped at a window, looking out. He spoke with his back to me.

"In reality, there is almost nothing you can do against misconduct, or even open felony crime, if it's committed by lawyers and judges," he said. "All the official complaint procedures you'll find at the courthouse or in the law books are a joke. Complaints about lawyers in Florida, go to the Bar Association, which is itself run by the judges and lawyers who are involved in the bribery of other judges and lawyers. Complaints about judges go to other judges, their friends. Nearly all complaints about judges and lawyers, thousands of them, are kept secret. Nearly all are dismissed or ignored. They are generally only used if the judges or politicians want to destroy someone. Some radical minority lawyer, or someone who isn't playing the bribery game. Somebody who has dared to expose wrongdoing. Otherwise, even criminal acts by lawyers and judges get a smiling cover-up."

"You're right," I said. "I had no idea it was this bad."

"It gets worse," he said. You won't find any lawyer to help you sue another lawyer for wrongdoing. They are too afraid of revenge by the judges. The police and even the FBI won't help you either. They all know the bribery game, they rely on the same judges to help send innocent people to jail. The more crooked the judge, the more eager he will be to help the police or the FBI do a dirty deal. The newspapers and other media won't help you. They hear these stories all the time. If they publish or broadcast your story, then they will have problems the next time they get sued. Or they might find themselves arrested on false charges."

"The media too?" I asked, incredulously.

"The newspapers are so tied into the establishment of judges and lawyers, that they sometimes help them commit crimes. They unfairly attack the victims. They've even helped plant false evidence in court cases. They help the legal establishment destroy innocent people. Even if they aren't harming you, they are afraid to help you, afraid of revenge if they expose judicial corruption."

"You're depressing me," I said.

"I'm not finished yet," he said. "Politicians won't help you either. Many of them were lawyers themselves, very used to the whole game of bribery with judges and other lawyers. The politicians accept the crooked courts as the way America is run. It helps the two parties to monopolize the political scene and prevent alternative movements from getting started. America's two party system is just another phony game like America's courts. These two parties pretend to argue over emotional issues like gun control and abortion, but in the end they both serve the big corporations. Half of us are still fooled. We think they represent us. The other half sense it's all phony, but feel helpless and don't know what to do. That's why many don't vote anymore. They feel helpless and hopeless in America."

"What about civil liberties or human rights groups?" I asked. "There's got to be something we can do."

"You can forget that," he said. "Most of them are just money raising groups that don't help the victims. Many are tied to one political party or the other. They are all afraid of the legal system. They can't get a lawyer to help them, either. They are without the resources or clout or media access to expose or change what is happening."

"I'm a bit surprised that you're telling me all this," I said. "You are a part of it."

"I've had enough," he said. "I've got a chance to effect real change, at least on a small level. I can't save the world, but maybe I can help here in Lee and Charlotte County. If you will help me win office."

"Why now?" I asked. "You've been an officer of the court for a long time."

"It wasn't always this bad," he said. "It was rare even, but as more and more judge and lawyers get away with blatant crimes, they are getting more open about it. They commit crimes in broad daylight. They know that no one will stop them. It's important for you to know, that once you start making accusations about legal corruption, you become an outlaw. You're fair game to be arrested on false charges. No lawyer will defend you. You'll be at the mercy of a thoroughly corrupt system. You may be trapped in a nightmare from which there is no escape, unless you run and hide."

"I know a thing or two about running and hiding," I said. "But what about you?"

"I've had a long and distinguished career here," he said. "Other than that Fiore deal, I'm clean. My credentials for office are impeccable. Maybe from there, I can do some real good."

"In the meantime, what do I do about Taylor Ford?" I asked. "She's part of our deal, like it or not."

"I've been giving that a great deal of thought," he said. "I'll need your help."

"You've got a plan?" I asked.

"I don't think we should discuss it here," he said. "Call me tomorrow. We'll meet somewhere else."

"Shall I bring a big fat check?" I asked.

"Payable to *Russell for Representative*," he said. "If you don't mind."

Fifteen

Jimi and I had given birth to our very own politician. Starting his campaign fund would drain our PAC's account, but we were getting new donations every day. Disclosure laws would reveal who was giving him money. We couldn't get around that. I hoped that his announcement speech would placate all of our activist friends. If he ran on the two issues we'd been hammering away at, he would attract plenty of his own supporters. If he helped me take down Taylor, I was willing to help him however I could.

Jimi and Holly were anxious to hear my report. I replayed our discussion, skipping over a lot of the deep corruption parts. Russell had made it seem impossible to correct. The truth was, I didn't even care. I just wanted Taylor to suffer. Jimi wanted to save his own hide.

There'd been no word from Beruff, but I had some red meat to throw to potential donors. A new name in the political game was going to shake things up. We'd encouraged someone to run for office that was honestly committed to our causes. Jimi spent that evening spreading rumors on the internet. The activist crowd was all agog at the possibilities. They were tired of holding signs in front of the courthouse or on the pier at Fort Myers Beach. They wanted some action.

After I filled in the details, Holly pulled me away from Jimi. We walked to the pool to talk.

"You're letting this thing consume you," she warned. "I think you should lighten up a little. Have some fun."

I ignored her at first, but she persisted. I was traveling in the wrong world, a place where I didn't belong. I belonged on my boat, out there on the sea. I should get away from this stress and bullshit. I just carried on about how we'd accomplished so much, and how we'd influenced a small part of the world.

She shoved me in the pool, fancy suit and all. She dove in after me, dunking my head as soon as I came up for air.

"You're Breeze, damn it," she said. "You're not Winston Shade."

"Okay, okay, I give up," I said. "You win. What do you want to do?"

"Let's get out of here for a few days," she suggested. "Take me out to Pelican Bay. We'll hang on the beach and count the stars."

"Taylor has eyes on the place," I said.

"We'll take my boat," she said. "It will be ready soon."

"I'm sorry to have forgotten about your boat," I said. "My bad."

"You've had your head up your ass," she said. "Taylor this, Taylor that."

"I sincerely apologize," I said. "Really. I'm sorry. Do you want me to just forget about the whole thing?"

"I'd never ask you to do that," she said. "I know how you are when you're on a mission."

"This one seems to have gotten out of hand," I admitted.

"That must be why I'm here," she said. "To provide you with some perspective."

"The world turns in mysterious ways," I said.

"Ain't that the truth," she said.

I dropped Holly at the boat yard on my way to meet Russell again. She'd clean up *Another Adventure* and make her ready to sail to Pelican Bay. I was looking forward to it, but I had business to take care of first.

Our meeting took place in a small café in downtown Fort Myers. Russell was rushed. He kept looking around the place. The check I handed him calmed his nerves.

"What's our plan for Taylor?" I asked.

"We set her up," he said.

"How so?" I asked.

"We send her a fake defendant," he said. "Arrest reports, criminal record, the whole nine yards."

"How do we know she'll pay a bribe on this person's behalf?" I asked.

"You'll have to get creative there," he said. "I'll have the cooperation of the judge beforehand."

"Leigh Hayes?" I asked.

"That's right," he said. "If she doesn't cooperate, I'll spill the beans on her."

"So Taylor will have a judge that's she's bribed in the past," I said. "And I have to find a defendant that is willing to suggest she do it again."

"And has the money to pay it," he said. "Not some low level drug dealer."

I laughed. I couldn't tell Russell that I'd once been a low level drug dealer who'd had enough money to bribe a judge, all facilitated by Taylor.

"Where am I supposed to find this person?" I asked.

"I told you I'd need your help," he said.

"Don't you guys have some informant or someone who can do the job?" I asked.

"I have to worry about entrapment," he said. "You bring me the defendant. I'll see that nothing happens to them. The FBI knows what we're going to do."

I wasn't sure how I was going to find someone. Jimi couldn't do it, for obvious reasons. Taylor and Holly had met. Taylor would smell a rat if Holly came in looking to bribe a judge. I drove back to the marina worrying about it. After I took off my Winston Shade outfit, I felt better. I was going to sail away for a few days. I needed it more than ever.

Once we cleared the lock, Holly started raising sails. We raced down the Myakka River and out into Charlotte Harbor. *Another Adventure* was truly a fine sailing vessel. Holly knew how to get the most out of her. The faster we went, the bigger Holly's smile became. This was when she was in her glory. When those sails were full of wind, nothing else mattered.

She didn't lower the sails when we made our approach to Pelican Bay. The entrance was narrow and a little tricky, but Holly didn't care. We sailed right into the bay, weaving through the anchored boats like a skier on a slalom course. She fell off the wind, dropped the sails and coasted to a stop. As the wind started driving us back, she lowered the anchor. We got a little sideways dropping back, as sailboats tend to do, but the anchor dug in and we straightened out nicely.

"Nice job, sailor girl," I said.

"Thanks, Captain," she said. "Let's hit the beach."

I lowered the dinghy and off we went. We chose the southern half of the island. There would be few, if any, people down there. We didn't swim. We just walked along the surf. I had concerns about getting in the water here. All the crap coming down the Caloosahatchee had raised bacteria levels all along the coast. I wasn't sure if it had made it this far north, but I wasn't taking any chances.

"Tell me again what happened with your boyfriend," I said.

"My faith in humanity is pretty weak right now," she said. "He was always telling me that I wasn't opening up, that I wasn't letting him in. Then he goes berserk and I find out he was seeing another chick. He was on her boat and screwing before the dust settled."

"Pretty shitty way to treat a lady," I said. "Young and dumb, I guess. Why did you take a chance on someone so young, anyway?"

"I seem to remember an older guy taking a young girl under his wing," she said. "That worked out pretty well. I suppose I was trying to emulate you."

"That's a first," I said. "I'm not sure I'm the best person to model your life after."

"It was a subconscious thing," she said. "I've got the benefit of hindsight now."

"Sorry it didn't work out better for you," I said.

"He was just an immature dick," she said. "His loss. Now tell me, what the hell are you doing up here?"

"This is home," I said. "It's where I go when I need to regroup."

"Not that," she said. "I mean what are you doing involving yourself in all this land-based drama?"

"The bad guys are on land this time," I said. "And the people I need to help me."

"I just don't get it," she said. "Politics, activism, it's not your turf, so to speak."

"That's why I invented Winston Shade," I said.

"Which is kind of creepy, if you ask me," she said.

"That's not what you said the other night," I said, laughing.

"Got me there," she admitted. "It was fun to fantasize about being with someone like him. Never going to happen in the real world."

"Why do you say that?" I asked. "You can get any man you want."

"Men are a mystery to me," she said. "Even sailors. All of them are assholes."

"Present company included?" I asked.

"You are different than other men," she said. "But we still couldn't work it out. I mean, being together long term."

"Does that make me an asshole?" I asked.

"Only if I'm an asshole too," she said. "I ran away just like you did."

"Should we rethink our choices?" I asked. "Is that what we're doing?"

"I would like to think less," she said. "I just want to be."

"You do a great job of being yourself," I said. "More than most."

"I'll take that as a compliment," she said. "No one is better at being their own person than you."

"I never planned it that way," I said. "It just happened. I've made so many wrong turns in my life. Hard to recall how I even got here."

"Regrets?" she asked.

"Only minor ones," I said. "I've done things my own way. It's worked out okay in the long run."

"I try," she said. "But I keep thinking that I'm wasting my life. That I need goals. I've got no purpose. I don't have your mastery of the *shit works out* attitude."

"It does work out," I said. "Maybe not the way you thought it would, but shit works out, one way or another."

"Maybe the student hasn't completed her lessons," she said.

"I'm no teacher," I said. "Don't take my ramblings as gospel."

"I can't stay here anyway," she said.

"No? Where will you go?" I asked.

"Back to the Keys," she said. "There's work doing boat bottoms there. I made enough contacts to keep me busy. I'll bounce from Key West to Marathon to Miami."

"Any plans to go back to the Bahamas?" I asked.

"I don't know," she said. "I won't go alone. Learned my lesson on that."

"What happened out there?" I asked.

"I was just lonely," she said. "The sailing was great. The water was awesome, but not having someone to share it with took away from the enjoyment."

"So you turned around and came back to Florida?" I asked.

"Yep," she said. "And jumped right into a stupid relationship. I let the loneliness get the best of me."

"I get lonely too," I said. "But I've come to terms with being alone. Sometimes it's just better that way."

"I'm starting to feel the same way," she said.

"For right now," I said. "Let's be alone together."

"While it lasts," she said. "Thanks, Breeze."

We spent the next few days fishing and walking the beach. We laid on deck at night and watched the stars. Holly blew her conch horn at sunset. We listened to the breath of dolphins as we drank our coffee in the mornings. We asked for nothing from each other. We were alone, but we were together. Sometimes that's all a person needs.

I knew that Holly was ready to leave. She had a life to begin down in the Keys. I had a lot on my plate. We were quiet on the trip back. Back at the dock, I was the first to speak.

"I could use some moral support," I said. "If you need a reason to stay a while longer."

"I am worried about you," she said. "This could go wrong in so many ways. You might need me around to pick up the pieces. But don't be surprised if I disappear."

"I understand," I said.

I understood all too well. I had a long history of disappearing when things got too complicated. It was my standard method of dealing with chaos. Maybe I'd bitten off more than I could chew this time. Things were certainly complicated. I couldn't give up now, though. I'd invested my life, and Jimi's life, in taking down Taylor. If we didn't succeed, she'd take us down instead. I was past the point of no return. Maybe it would be better for Holly to leave. I didn't want her to become collateral damage.

Jimi hit me with a long list of matters that needed my attention as soon as I returned. Stephen Russell was soon to make his candidacy known to the public. He was going to make a speech and I needed to be there. Carlos Beruff had finally called. He wanted to meet. Several more big money donors had called. Jimi's social media campaign had created more interest than we could handle. I was rested from my mini vacation. My head was clear. I donned my Winston Shade veneer and prepared for battle.

I called Beruff. He agreed to meet, but on his terms. He clearly wanted to take control. I sensed that he wanted to use me more than I wanted to use him. He was a lot better at the game than I was. I had to drive up to Bradenton for our talk. We met in a dark bar on a side street, far from prying eyes.

"If it ain't the king of clean water," he said. "Your little group is making a lot of waves."

"And attracting donors," I said. "We'll announce our first endorsement very soon."

"About that," he said. "You and I both know that I don't have a prayer in this election. It's more about setting myself up for the future."

"I can appreciate that," I said, not knowing where he was going.

"I can't sign on to this clean water stuff," he said. "People aren't that dumb. I'm a developer for Christ's sake. I bulldoze mangroves and dig canals in sensitive areas. It'll never fly."

"I'm sorry to hear that," I said. "Protecting the environment is our first priority."

"I'm curious about that other thing," he said. "The lawyer lady."

"She's a personal priority," I said.

"What gave you a hard-on for her?" he asked. "Why should I care?"

"It's a long story, but it involves murder for hire," I told him. "She involved me without my knowledge. She set me up to get a friend killed, among others. She was behind the theft of your offshore funds."

"She just got all that money back," he said. "We're square with her."

"I got your money back," I told him. "I found the guy who took it. I convinced him to return it. She wants to kill him anyway."

"You're not who you say you are," he said.

"No I'm not," I admitted. "I worked with Taylor. She used me to find people, so she could kill them."

"That's a serious accusation," he said. "Not the kind of stuff an aspiring politician should involve himself in."

"I still plan to take her down," I said. "With or without your help."

"You got a plan?" he asked.

"I've been working with the State's Attorney," I said. "We hope to introduce her to a fake defendant. Get her to bribe a judge again, except this time the law steps in and pops her."

"She doesn't throw bribes around for every Tom, Dick and Harry that comes through her office," he said.

"I realize that," I said. "We need someone with a little gravitas to pull it off."

"Maybe that's where I can help," he said.

"You?" I asked.

"Not me," he said. "One of my guys. Then I make it known I want to pay his way out."

"She's done it for you before," I said.

"Exactly," he said. "I'm a somebody. She'll bite."

"And what do you want in return?" I asked.

"Your cash for the bribe," he said. "And an equal amount to my campaign."

"I can't let Independent Florida give money to an anti-environmental candidate," I said. "It would seriously harm our efforts."

"You run it through a shell group," he said. "I've got lots of shell companies. We move money around enough to make you dizzy looking for it."

"Not my area of expertise," I said.

"I got a guy," he said. "I'll have him get in touch with you."

"Why are you agreeing to all this?" I asked. "What's your interest here?"

"I like to stay on top of things in my little kingdom," he said. "That lawyer is getting too big for her britches. I may be crooked, but there's no trail of bodies. I think it's time to put a stop to her little enterprise."

"I appreciate it," I said. "I hope I'm not making a deal with the devil here."

"I'm no devil," he said. "But if I need your help in the future, you'll help. Understood?"

"I think so," I said. "Quid Pro Quo."

"Scratch my back," he said.

Sixteen

I left the meeting with Beruff feeling dirty. I hadn't sold out the principles of Independent Florida, but I sold a little of my soul. I hoped I had enough of myself left to make it through this ordeal. I used a little mental gymnastics to transfer the blame away from Meade Breeze and onto Winston Shade.

By the time I got back to the marina, Beruff's guy had already called. He set up a meeting with Jimi to help us create the shell companies we needed to route money to Beruff without disclosing it as a direct donation from Independent Florida. His name was John Muller. He was a long-time employee of Beruff's. He made his living creating fake companies and moving money around. When his employer's construction company was under fire for building homes with contaminated drywall, he'd made it look like bankruptcy was imminent. The money was simply shuffled around and laundered through various shell companies, also owned by his boss.

Once his work was complete, he told us he had an additional reason for the meeting.

"Boss man says I'm going to be your fall guy," he stated.

"Our fake defendant?" I asked. "You're willing to be part of our trap?"

"Willing's got nothing to do with it," he said. "Boss says go. I go."

"You won't have any trouble," I told him. "We've got the State's Attorney behind the whole scheme."

"I've got a bone to pick with that lady lawyer myself," he said. "It will be my pleasure to watch her squirm."

"What's your deal with her?" I asked.

"I'm not really an accountant," he said. "Not even a financial advisor. I'm the computer guy, but I move all this money around, hiding it from taxes and so forth. She got to us with this Jimi D. business. I take it personally."

"You still have a grudge against me?" asked Jimi. "I came clean. The money's all been repaid."

"We figure that hot little bitch used you," John said. "But that's now. We would have worked to bring you to justice if you hadn't turned up with the money. Our kind of justice."

"So now you're focusing your anger towards her?" asked Jimi.

"Yea, but we can't just go in and pop a lawyer," he said. "We'll help you do it your way."

We ended our meeting with tentative handshakes. He was a crusty old fellow, pushing eighty I figured. He'd worked for Beruff for a long time. I bet he'd seen a lot go down over the years. We'd decided to work up some money laundering and wire fraud charges against him. Russell would handle that end of the sting.

Speaking of Russel, next on our agenda was his announcement speech. I drove to Fort Myers the next day to be in attendance. I was not part of the ceremony. I didn't want Taylor to see Winston Shade on the news. I'd been lucky so far. Apparently, she'd been too preoccupied to care about the clean water movement.

Stephen Russell stood atop the courthouse steps. Press microphones surrounded his podium. Members of the media filled the first few rows, but scores of clean water activist outnumbered them. We'd asked every group we'd donated to, to send as many members as they could, promising good news. It was an impressive turnout. Russell sounded confident.

My name is Stephen Russell, and I'm here today to announce my candidacy for the Florida House of Representatives. I have a long, successful record as a prosecutor and State's Attorney right here in Southwest Florida. Soon you'll be hearing about an aggressive campaign to root out corruption in our justice system. Many of you feel that the system no longer represents you, the people. I'm dedicated to changing that perception.

But that's not all I want to talk about today. I want to talk about clean water as a basic human right.

The crowd applauded loudly, halting his speech for several minutes.

Our once beautiful waters are under attack. Our tourism based economy is under attack. For decades, politicians have promised to solve the problem, all the while taking millions from Big Sugar and turning a blind eye. The Lake O discharges must stop. We must send the water south. We must buy the land that was promised in Amendment One.

Again, the crowd went wild. They stomped their feet in unison and chanted "Buy the land, buy the land." They continued for five minutes, until Russell raised his arms. Once they calmed down, he resumed speaking.

I was born and raised here, and I'm proud of it. Our rivers and beaches are a national treasure. The Everglades is a national treasure. Your politicians have not been good stewards of these amazing resources. I say we kick them all out. Every sitting politician that's taken money from Big Sugar has to go.

The applause was deafening. The crowd took up a new chant. "Kick them out," they yelled, over and over again. Finally, Russell raised his arms again. The crowd obeyed his command. He didn't exactly have charisma in the traditional sense. He had a serious demeanor. I felt that these were serious times. The crowd didn't want pretty promises. They wanted someone who would take action, get things done. Russell sounded like he'd make it happen.

I stand before you today, thanks to the endorsement of Independent Florida. I admire the work they've done to raise awareness of our water quality issues. I know a lot of you are concerned citizens on this matter. I've seen you at the demonstrations. I know you want your voice to be heard. I'm listening, Florida. I hear your cries.

The applause began anew, but Russell raised his hands immediately.

I also want to acknowledge the fine people of all the other groups who've been fighting this fight. Everglades Trust. Captains for Clean Water. Southwest Florida Citizens for Clean Water, and so on. I'm sorry I can't remember all of you, but I promise you this; you'll always have an open invitation to my office. Winning the fight for clean water is my number one priority. I'll need all of you to help if we are to win. My seat in the House of Representatives will be your seat. Thank you. Thank you all.

There was no stopping this round of applause. Russell had won over the activists with his first speech. He shook hands with many of them, before returning to his office inside the courthouse. I was proud of him. He'd stayed on message. There was no mention of divisive issues. He made no stand on gay marriage, abortion, or trans-gender bathrooms. He was a two-issue candidate. He'd tackle corruption. He'd fight for clean water. He came across as straight-forward and honest. He was serious, but he truly cared about those two issues. I thought it was a winning formula.

I raced back to the marina to marshal the troops, all three of us. I sent quick communications to all the associated groups, asking them to donate to the Russell campaign. We each used our multiple social media accounts to rave about the speech. We turned his announcement into the number one trending news story in Florida. I was truly amazed by the power of the internet. It was not something I was familiar with. I had no idea we could ever accomplish so much. Jimi used his laptop and shared it with me. Holly used her phone exclusively.

It was more than just three people sitting on a boat though. The people of south Florida, on both coasts, were fed up. Even with all the national hub-bub about Donald Trump and Hillary Clinton, the number one concern here was the death of our waterways. Thousands of ordinary citizens were moved to become activists. Demonstrations were being held from Fort Myers Beach on the west coast, to Stuart on the east coast. More and more stories circulated on Facebook, educating more and more people to the imminent danger they faced. Flesh-eating bacteria made its presence known. Beaches were closed. Water samples were sent to Congress and the governor's office. Blue-green algae worked its way through the locks and towards the coast. Indian River Lagoon was plagued with dozens of manatee deaths. Fish kills were the norm. Sea grass beds were dying off at an alarming rate. Shell fishing was banned in Pine Island Sound.

Stephen Russell was out in front of the movement, but he hadn't forgotten my other priority. We were still on track to nail Taylor to the wall, but he had additional targets as well. He was quietly building cases against a dozen lawyers and an equal number of judges. Exposing wide-spread corruption during election season would seriously boost his credentials as a candidate. It was in his hands now. I introduced him to John Muller and he took it from there.

I was really looking forward to stepping back from this operation, but there were more loose ends to tie up. Those mystery donors had made Independent Florida rich. Dozens of smaller donations came in daily. We need to send that money out into the battlefield to fulfill our mission statement. I didn't know where to start. I asked for advice from the leaders of the various groups we'd been dealing with.

Everglades Trust had started a new advertising campaign which endorsed candidates. "My Name is Will. Political Will," their ads said. I liked their non-partisan approach. It was a political problem, but not a partisan one. We followed their lead. Independent Florida first endorsed and donated to Representative Heather Fitzenhagen, a Republican in District 78. We also endorsed another Republican for Martin County Commission. We sent money to Jacqui Thurlow-Lippisch to help her win that job. We endorsed Democrat Patrick Murphy in his bid to unseat Marco Rubio. We threw our weight behind Chauncy Goss. His opponent, Francis Rooney, had deep ties to companies wishing to expand drilling for oil in sensitive areas.

Each endorsement was widely touted on social media. Donations were disclosed immediately. The Everglades Trust had plenty of clout, but our endorsements came with cash. Soon we were inundated with requests from candidates. Everyone wanted our endorsement, and our money. Not many of them earned it. It soon became impossible to find politicians who weren't influenced by Big Sugar.

Once we'd distributed enough of our donor's money, we were able to relax a bit. I hung out with Holly at the pool most afternoons. Jimi never seemed to come out of his boat. When he did, he carried his phone and his laptop wherever he went.

"How the hell did we end up driving a political movement?" he asked.

"It will all be over soon," I assured him.

"I'll be happy when Taylor's in jail," he said. "All this other stuff is just a distraction."

"You're doing good work, Jimi," I told him. "You should be proud."

"I've got a million bucks in the bank. I've got my boat. Here I sit working my ass off instead of enjoying paradise."

"You won't be able to enjoy anything if won't don't defeat Taylor," I reminded him.

"Let's get it over with," he said. "Tell Russell to get a move on."

"I'm confident that he's working on it," I said. "It's essential to his own plan."

"The fascinating mind of Meade Breeze," Holly interrupted. "You show up here nothing but a boat bum. Now you've got a high-ranking officer of the court working to settle a score with your ex-girlfriend. Impossible."

"Don't forget his alter ego," said Jimi. "He's a big player in south Florida politics."

"Blows my mind," Holly said. "I think I liked it better when you were chasing bad guys."

"I resemble that remark," said Jimi. "He's still chasing bad guys. The bad guy is Taylor."

"There's a fine line between bad guy and good guy in Breeze's world," she said.

"I can't disagree with that," I said. "Sometimes I'm not sure which side of the line I'm on."

"I'd say good guy," said Holly.

"Me too," said Jimi. "Mostly good guy, anyway."

I'd had this argument with myself on many occasions. I didn't set out to be a bad guy. Most of the time I wasn't. When I was selling my homegrown dope to suburban housewives, I never thought of it as a crime. Even after I was running pounds of the stuff to Marathon, who was I hurting? It was just a weed. I didn't smoke the stuff myself, but I knew plenty of people who did. Most of them were upstanding citizens living exemplary lives. They certainly weren't criminals.

Circumstances changed though. Money that was rightfully mine, had been sent to a different ex-girlfriend. I did not have the means to recover it. I needed fast cash. Running coke in the Keys did not make me a good guy. It took almost a year to escape that gig. All the coke I'd transported had most certainly done a lot of harm. Nothing I could do about it now. I'd also pulled a bunch of small time scams on married men who were cheating on their wives. Another woman had talked me into it. It ended with her death on a dirty street in Miami. I did my best not to think about that. I'd brought the killer to justice, but it didn't bring her back to life. Fine line indeed. I'd danced all over that line.

Even now, the money that I'd originally invested with Jimi was coke money. When I found him on Grand Cayman, he'd paid me off not to reveal his location. More ill-gotten gains. Now we were working together to ruin Taylor. Good guy or bad guy?

"I know you mean well," said Holly. "But when this is all over, you should really consider a new line of work."

"I didn't plan to get into this mess," I said. "Shit happens."

"Separate yourself from it all," she said. "Hop in that old trawler and make yourself scarce."

"That's exactly what I was trying to do when all this fell in my lap," I said.

"You didn't have to answer the call," she said. "You couldn't resist. It's who you are."

"Maybe you're right," I said.

Seventeen

Russell had worked out the details. The fake arrest records had gone on file. Judge Hayes was willing to cooperate. The FBI was standing by. John Muller hired Taylor Ford as his defense attorney. The wheels were in motion.

Carlos Beruff had a lunch meeting with Miss Ford. No money was exchanged, but he made his intentions clear. She didn't object.

The suspense was killing Jimi and I. Our workload had lightened considerably. We'd set the dominos falling and all we could do now was sit and watch them tumble into place. Holly was getting impatient for different reasons. There was nothing holding her. There was no real reason for her to stay. Our reunion had not sparked the fire that we'd fail to find the first time around. We cared for each other deeply, but it was apparent that we were destined to live our lives apart.

"Damn, Breeze," she said. "I want to see how this whole thing pans out, but I feel like I'm wasting my time here."

"I'll be sad to see you go," I said. "But I understand. You've got a life to lead."

"Maybe you should come to the Keys when this is over," she said. "Or at least tell me you might. That way it won't be goodbye forever."

"Okay," I said. "I might come to the Keys when this is over. Never know."

"Thanks."

I was summoned to Russell's office the next day. I was starting to hate putting on my monkey suit to play Winston Shade. It had been fun at first, but the seriousness of the situation wore on me. I waited for it to all fall apart at any time. Someone would see through my façade. It would all go to hell. All the groundwork would have been for nothing. I couldn't let that happen. I straightened my tie, combed my hair just right and walked the walk.

Russell was all business. He didn't even thank me for his successful campaign launch.

"I've got six solid cases working right now," he told me. "Another five maybes. I can't use the same trick on all of them. Once the first shoe drops everyone will be alert to what's going on."

"Then make Taylor the first shoe," I said. "I don't really care about the rest of them."

"I do," he countered. "Several of them are more egregious offenders than her."

"What are you getting at?" I asked.

"There's a distinct possibility that she'll roll over on her fellow officers of the court," he said.

"In exchange for leniency?" I asked. "She'll get a reduced sentence or something?"

"If she sings like a bird she'll avoid jail time," he said.

"You've got to be kidding me," I said. "That's unacceptable."

"She'll be disbarred," he said. "She'll be ruined in Florida."

"Other options?" I asked.

"We go after someone else first," he said. "Get them to roll on her. She'll go to jail, most likely."

"Problems?"

"We don't have the fake defendant," he said. "We've already got Taylor wrapped up. All we have to do is spring the trap. Everyone is ready to roll with the original plan."

"One more question," I said. "Does the Attorney General know what you're up to?"

"Pam Bondi?" he asked. "No. We are keeping Tallahassee out of this. At least for now. Why?"

"Taylor and Miss Bondi have made acquaintance," I told him. "Taylor got a previous investigation squelched."

"That's why we're leaving her out," he said. "But I'm curious as to how you know so much."

"I'd like to tell you that it's my business to know and how smart I am," I began. "But the truth is, Taylor and I were intimate. We were a couple, though she kept it quiet."

"Scuttlebutt was that she was screwing someone who was socially unacceptable," he said. "She wouldn't be seen with him in public."

"I am socially unacceptable," I said. "Or I was anyway."

"Maybe it's time that you come clean about exactly who you are," he said. "This is all about to go down. It's too important to let slip away now. What else don't I know?"

"Taylor bribed a judge on my behalf," I admitted. "I was arrested with a considerable amount of marijuana. More than enough for a charge of intent to distribute. I was able to buy my way out."

"I'm too far down your rabbit hole to arrest you now," he said. "We've thrown in together on this deal."

"You could arrest me as Meade Breeze," I said. "That's who I really am. Won't hurt your campaign."

"Meade Breeze," he said. "That name came up in our investigation. You were the only person we couldn't connect to someone in a position of power. How'd you manage to arrange the bribe?"

"I do know someone in a position of power," I told him. "But I will never reveal his identity."

"Someone I might know?" he asked.

"The general public wouldn't know his name," I said. "But he has his finger on the pulse of south Florida politics. He has a tremendous amount of pull with the judges too. He just stays out of the public eye."

"What's your connection to this mystery man?" he asked.

"Old boating buddies," I said. "Friends. Nothing political at all."

"You're just protecting an old friend?" he asked. "Is that it?"

"He's very connected to Big Sugar," I said. "You don't want his name anywhere near this mess."

"He's untouchable?" he asked.

"Last I knew he was out of the country," I said. "He lives on his yacht. Pulls strings from anywhere in the world."

"I'm trying to keep this all straight," said Russell. "You have a powerful mystery friend who influences Florida politics and has ties to Big Sugar. You were sleeping with the lawyer who arranged your bribe. You've become a huge champion of the clean water movement, which hates Big Sugar. I'm going to launch my campaign by arresting your ex-girlfriend. I can't know who this power player is. Is that about it?"

"I won't give up his name," I said. "No way, no how. You can arrest me right now, but I won't do it. In fact, I'll call him to help me get out of trouble. Probably won't go well for you. He's helped Taylor as well."

"So we leave that hornet's nest alone," he said. "What else is there that I should know?"

"Arrest Taylor first," I suggested. "There's more, but I'm not ready to reveal it yet. I want to see her face when she gets taken out."

"What if she walks?" he asked.

"Then I'll tell you what else I know," I said.

"Who are you, Meade Breeze?" he asked.

"I'm nobody," I told him. "Just a boat bum."

Russell chewed on that for a few minutes. I felt bad for jerking him around, but I'd already told him more than I thought I ever would. He'd taken my money to start his campaign. He'd taken my inside information to start his war on corruption. I was betting that he wouldn't turn on me. He was not a corrupt man, but he knew how the game was played. He had everything to gain by playing along.

"I'll get in touch with Beruff," he said. "We'll get the bribe to her. Then we wait for her to pay off Judge Hayes."

"I'd like to know when she's in custody," I said. "Keep me informed."

"I'm giving you a pass, you know," he said. "This was never about the people paying the bribes. It's always been about busting the lawyers and judges."

"I was counting on it," I said. "Otherwise you'd have to arrest people like Beruff. Could get real messy."

"I'll call when we have Miss Ford," he said.

Jimi and John Muller had set up a chain of subsidiaries to Independent Florida. We gave money to a group that sounded like it was pro-environment. That entity gave money to a group with an ambiguous purpose. That group gave money to something called Sustainable Development. Eventually, the cash made its way to one of Beruff's shell companies. John worked it through those channels until it was in his boss's control.

Carlos Beruff handed a manila envelope full of cash to Taylor Ford. John Muller was a faithful employee. He couldn't go to jail. Taylor understood. A mutual agreement was made. Taylor paid a visit to the chambers of Judge Leigh F. Hayes. She handed the judge the envelope. Hayes looked inside. The judge then pushed a button on her phone's intercom system. Deputies from the Sheriff's Department entered the room. Taylor was read her rights and led out of the courthouse in handcuffs.

I got the call from Russell. He'd been present at her arraignment, where she'd offered up testimony that implicated nearly every lawyer and judge in two counties. It was too big a prize for Russell to turn down. Taylor would eventually go free, in exchange for her complete cooperation.

I turned myself into Winston Shade and drove to downtown Fort Myers. Russell was waiting for me. Taylor was in the interrogation room.

"She's been the picture of composure," he said. "Very calm. Her only problem is the need to know who is responsible for upsetting the apple cart."

"Let's see how calm she is when she finds out," I suggested.

"You can't go in there alone," he said. "We'll need an officer, and I'll be there too."

The cop and Russell went in first. I could hear their conversation over a speaker in an observation room.

"I can't believe you're doing this," said Taylor to Russell. "You knew that Fiore case stunk to high heaven, and you got a promotion out of it. Why now?"

"More information has been brought to my attention," he said. "A concerned citizen with inside knowledge persuaded me to clean up the corruption in our local legal system."

"Who?" she asked. "What concerned citizen?"

"Winston Shade," he told her.

"The clean water guy?" she asked. "What's he got against me? We've never even met."

"I think maybe you have," he said.

That was my cue. I strode into the room with my head held high and my chest out.

"Hello, Taylor," I said.

She lost all composure. Fire shot out of her eyes. She made fists with both hands and started screaming in an evil tone of voice.

"That's not Winston Shade," she yelled. "That's Meade Breeze. He's nothing. He's nobody. He's just a lowlife boat bum."

She came across the desk and launched herself at me. The cop intercepted her just in time. She continued screaming hysterically as she tried to gouge out my eyes. The lady made a spectacle of herself, calling me every profanity she could think of. The officer was a bit too gentle and she wriggled away. Her hair was a mess. It gave her a Medusa look as she continued ranting wildly. Spit flew out of her mouth with every invective she hurled at me.

When the cop tried to regain control, she struck him with both fists. He shot a quick glance at Russell, who nodded yes. Taylor was on the floor with her hands behind her back in a flash. The cop had a knee planted firmly in her back and a handful of hair. She continued to cuss my name and my existence, but added a few choice words for the cop too.

"I believe that warrants a charge of assaulting an officer," said Russell. "Lock her up. Come get me when she calms down."

He called another officer to assist with her transport. She continued kicking all the way down the hall. When she was out of sight, Russell turned to me with a curious expression.

"Did you know she'd react that way?" he asked. "We can probably get her a few months for that little display."

"I couldn't predict what she would do," I said. "But she's clearly unstable. I guess I didn't really know her at all."

"You certainly burst her bubble," he said, laughing. "That bitch is nuts."

"Don't underestimate her," I warned. "She'll calm down. She's smart and devious. Stay one step ahead of her."

"I hope she calms down," he said. "The testimony of a raving lunatic won't help us at all."

"She'll do whatever she has to do to stay out of jail," I said.

"She's not going anywhere for a while," he said. "Let's see if she lawyers up. I can use the additional charge or charges as leverage."

"I'll need to know immediately if she walks out of here," I said. "My personal safety depends on it."

"You think she'll come after you?" he asked.

"Or send someone for me," I said. "This side of her I know all about."

"You're still holding back on me, aren't you?" he asked.

"Never show all your cards at once," I replied.

"Call me when you're ready to talk," he said. "In the meantime, I'll let you know if she walks."

Winston Shade had walked into that courthouse. Meade Breeze walked out. I purposely messed up my hair, vowing not to cut it until any semblance of style was gone. I took off my tie and threw it out the window. It was time to return the Lexus. I was done pretending to be someone I was not. I could never live in Taylor's world, or even Russell's.

I was very pleasantly surprised to learn that Holly was still at the marina. She hadn't left for the Keys. I almost ran to her before giving her a big hug.

"Is it over?" she asked.

"Not yet," I said. "Far from it, but she's been arrested. She flipped out when I walked in as Winston Shade. Completely lost it."

"Hell has no fury," she said. "Woman scorned and all that."

"Bat shit crazy is what she is," I said. "How did I not see that before?"

"You weren't thinking with your big brain," she said. "All you saw was how hot she was."

"Maybe," I said. "Wouldn't be the first time, but I think realizing it was me that doomed her caused her to snap."

"Either way, you won," she said. "Breeze one, Taylor zero."

"I just hope there aren't too many innings left in this ballgame," I said. "I'm getting the itch to move on from this place."

"Me too," she said. "Let's just ditch this joint and sail away."

"Soon," I said. "I have to see this thing through."

I could see the disappointment in her eyes, but she didn't speak of it. We both went to Jimi's boat to tell him the news. He was busy clacking away at his laptop.

"Relax, Jimi," I told him. "Take a break. Taylor's in lockup."

"A clean water warrior's job is never done," he said. "We've created a monster."

"You might want to think about winding down Independent Florida," I suggested. "When the dust clears from this, I'm taking off."

"Me too," said Holly.

"What am I supposed to do then?" asked Jimi.

"You have a boat," I said. "Go wherever you want."

"I don't know where I'd go," he said.

"I'm going to the Keys," said Holly. "You're welcome to follow me down."

She looked at me, waiting for me to say that I was going to the Keys too.

"I'll go down with you," I said. "But no promises. We'll see how it goes."

Holly and Jimi spoke in unison.

"Great," they said.

We were all smiles.

Eighteen

A few days in jail caused Taylor to settle down. She combined a spirit of cooperation with veiled threats in an attempt to gain any advantage. She threw me under the bus, of course, but it didn't deter Russell. She even implied that he had some skeletons in his closet that she knew about, but he didn't flinch. Apparently, he really was clean, other than his complicity in the Fiore case. If she tried to bring that up in court, it would only convince the court of her own guilt.

She chose to represent herself, as was her right. To be honest, she wouldn't find a better lawyer to defend her. She was tainted goods in the law profession. No one would touch her case. She tried to use some arcane eighteenth century law to muddy the waters. Since her accuser wasn't who he said he was, she'd been denied her right to face him. It didn't fly. She was up against it, and she knew it. There was nothing left for her to do but cooperate.

Russell got everything he needed and more. Taylor turned into a marvelous informant. She provided so much value to Russell that he agreed to let her go. The additional charges stemming from her assault of an officer were dropped. The disbarment procedure was underway. She had agreed not to dispute it, as part of her deal with Russell. She was finished as a lawyer, at least in Florida. She wouldn't be able to find a job as a clerk.

I should have been happy with the outcome, but I wasn't satisfied. It was time to give Russell more. I used Jimi's car to drive back to Fort Myers. I was not dressed as Winston Shade. I entered Russell's office wearing shorts, a tank top, and flip flops. The shorts had some holes in them. The shirt had an oil stain. My ball cap was faded by the sun. Salt stained the brim.

"What do you have for me, Breeze?" asked Russell.

"Attempted murder, times two," I said. "Maybe even three."

"Whoa, now," he said. "Where did that come from?"

"There's a bunch of financial stuff too," I added. "Not sure what's legal and what's not."

"Start at the beginning," he said.

I took a deep breath and gathered my thoughts. The road had been a long and winding one. It most likely began while Taylor and I were still together. I was mixed up in her affairs like a bee in a hive.

"It started with those guys that paid the bribes," I began. "Taylor identified people with the means and money. She targeted them for a financial scheme. She used a formally legitimate financial advisor, whose trust she won with her feminine charms, to gather up a large sum of money to be deposited in offshore tax havens. Her ultimate goal was to acquire all the money herself, leaving the advisor holding the bag."

"But something went wrong," surmised Russell.

"The advisor figured out he was being played," I said. "He took the money and ran."

"Nothing for me to go on, without him or the money," he said.

"That's where I came in," I said. "I invested money with him also, at Taylor's suggestion. When I found out that all the money was gone, I hunted him down."

"Where was he?" he asked.

"Grand Cayman," I answered.

"How'd you find him there?" he asked.

"It's what I do," I said. "Long story. Anyway, I found him and got my money back."

"What about the rest of it?" he asked.

"I didn't care about the rest of it," I said. "As a matter of fact, the guy paid me to keep his location a secret. I made out pretty well."

"Who is this guy?" he asked.

"I'll get to that," I said. "Moving on, Taylor paid me to run down another guy in the Bahamas. He as the bookkeeper for one of the patsies she'd stolen the money from. They blamed him for giving the money to the advisor."

"Did you find him?" he asked.

"I did find him, but quickly had second thoughts," I admitted.

"Why was that?" he asked.

"I figured out that they planned to execute the man," I said. "Taylor used me to find him, then I was to call in the goons. He was a dead man if I turned him over to them. Instead, I helped him run."

"Where's he at now?" he said. "We might need him eventually."

"He's fine and back with his employer," I said. "I got the advisor to pay back what he'd taken from his boss. Made it look like the bookkeeper was a hero, tracking down the money and all."

"So you were still in touch with the financial advisor?" he asked.

"At that point I was," I answered. "But he relocated soon afterwards. I didn't know where he was after that."

"So maybe Taylor was involved in a murder for hire scheme," he said. "But the hit never went down thanks to your intervention, even though you were the one who found the bookkeeper in the first place. Possibly one attempted murder, but slim, especially without the particulars to testify."

"Jimi D. resurfaced," I said.

"Jimi D.?" he asked.

"That's his name," I told him. "Jimi D. was the financial advisor that disappeared with all the money."

"What do you mean he resurfaced?" he asked.

"He came to me," I said. "He wanted to pay back all the money. At the same time, Taylor wanted to hire me to track him down again. She was sure I knew where he was."

"Didn't you?"

"Yes, but she didn't really know that," I said. "I saw an easy payday, but I also smelled a rat."

"Because she wanted to kill this Jimi guy?"

"She tried to pay me just to find him. I said I'd get the money," I explained. "We dickered over the details."

"You already knew he wanted to give the money back. You just didn't want Taylor to know where he was."

"Exactly," I said. "I made a deal with him down in Grand Cayman. It was still in effect as far as I was concerned."

"How much?" Russell asked.

"How much what?"

"How much did he pay you to keep your mouth shut?"

"Two hundred grand," I said.

"You lead a strange life, Mr. Breeze," he said.

"That's beside the point," I said. "Taylor wanted to kill him. She had people follow me, hoping that I would lead them to him."

"Did they ever find him?"

"Almost," I said. "We were on our boats in Fort Myers Beach when they came looking."

"Any violence? Shots fired? Any overt attempt on his life?"

"No, but the guy was armed," I said. "We disarmed him. He was there to kill Jimi if he found him."

"This is all fascinating," he said. "There's another dimension to this world that I never see, and I'm the State's Attorney. I just can't justify charges on what you're telling me. There's no evidence, only hearsay."

"How do we substantiate all these events?" I asked. "There's a clear pattern to her behavior."

"I'd have to brush up on malfeasance law," he said. "Unlawful activity by a public official has different guidelines than for the general public. Might be something there, but I've already made a deal with her on the bribery scandal."

"There's got to be a way you can nail her," I said. "I wouldn't put it past her to come after me or Jimi, now that she's free."

"Does she know where you are?" he asked.

"I don't think so," I said. "But she obviously knows I'm local. Only a matter of time before she finds me."

"Why don't you just leave?"

"I had planned to," I said. "But I want to see this through. Let's lock her up."

"Easier said than done," he said. "She's just had her brush with the law. I can't believe she'd turn around and try to make a move on you so soon."

"You don't know her like I do."

"You're being paranoid," he said.

"It keeps me alive," I countered. "It's not paranoia when they're really after you."

"Let me confer with some of my colleagues," he said. "Everyone has been kept pretty busy wrapping up the bribery investigation. We'll try to find an angle. In the meantime, keep your head down."

"That's the plan," I said. "Don't let this drag on too long. If I need to disappear, I will, but I'd really like to see this out."

"I think I can understand why you want to go after her so hard," he said. "But you're up to your ass in illegality in all of this. You'd be a terrible witness. The defense would eat you alive."

"Then don't let it come to that," I said. "I've got faith in you. You're smart. You'll figure something out."

With that statement, I turned and walked out. I was still holding on to my "shit works out" theory. I was disappointed, but I'd done what I could do, for now.

I started considering the reasons for my lust for revenge. It's normal to want payback when someone harms you. Had Taylor actually harmed me? I'd outsmarted her for the most part. I'd stayed one step ahead. Physically, I was completely unharmed. Mentally? Emotionally? What damage had I suffered as a result of her actions?

If I was hurt because I'd failed to realize how bad of a person she was, wasn't that my own fault? I had a hard time blaming myself on that score. She'd thrown her bags on my boat one day and asked me to take her away from it all. I'd be so close to fulfilling my dreams. I thought I was on my way to spending my life in the islands with a beautiful woman at my side. She took that away from me. She hated my lifestyle. She couldn't hack it.

That was one aspect, but the truth was that she had used me. She used me by telling me to trust Jimi with my money. She used me to track down that poor bookkeeper. She used me to track down Jimi. Everything had been a lie. She never cared for me from the start. Maybe she enjoyed the sex, but it was a tool to keep me compliant. She used it to control me. She kept me blind to her true intentions. I was nothing but a pawn in a kingdom that she ruled over. That really pissed me off.

I gave her a fair trial in my mind. I found her guilty. She was guilty of Abuse of Breeze. No forgiveness could be found. A grudge would be carried eternally, even after punishment had been meted out.

I had a good man working on a legal path to bring her to justice. I truly believed that Russell was a good man, a good steward of the law, but he was handicapped by the law as well. I was not. Maybe I could come up with a way to take matter into my own hands. I drove back to the marina to discuss it with my two friends.

I found Jimi and Holly at the pool. For the first time in a long time, Jimi did not have his laptop. He was on a chaise lounge in the shade. His hat was pulled down over his face. Holly was floating on a pool noodle, drink in hand. Matt and Bruce were in the pool too. The scene made me wish for normalcy in my life. Why couldn't I just stay here and drink beer in the pool? I could have some real friends. I could lead a normal life.

I knew that wasn't going to happen. I was destined to lurk on the fringes of polite society. I'd make my way on my wits and the will of the sea. That's who I was. That's who I'd remain. I adored Holly, but I wasn't responsible for her happiness. Jimi and I had become friends, but he'd have to find his own way as well.

The time was approaching for me to ride off into the sunset, but I had a score to settle first. I'd finish this business, with or without Holly and Jimi.

"What's up, Breeze?" asked Holly. "How'd things go with Russell?"

"He listened," I said. "He'll work on it."

"You don't sound impressed," she said.

"I'm thinking I may have to act on my own," I told her.

"What about us?" she asked.

"I don't want to put either of you in danger," I said. "Ultimately, it's my cross to bear."

"Ooh, listen to the poor martyr," she said. "Breeze carries the weight of the world. You've got friends now. We're the three amigos."

"One for all, and all for one," chimed in Jimi. "I started this mess. I should help clean it up."

"As long as I'm here," said Holly. "You can count me in."

So we were a team. The Three Amigos of Palm Island Marina bonded over beers. It felt good. We all retreated to our own boats as the bugs set in after sunset. We didn't solve the world's problems. We didn't even solve how to finish Taylor, but we cemented our friendship in a very satisfying way. I felt confident that together we'd accomplish our mission. Now that I had teammates, Taylor was in deeper shit than ever.

Sleepiness overcame me before I could figure out how to best utilize my new team. It was a night of deep sleep and disturbing dreams. I was on the streets of Miami, running towards a madman with a gun. He aimed and fired. I ran at him harder. He fired again before I dealt him a crushing blow. I pounded away at him there on the pavement. Joy lay bleeding behind me. I got to her in time to watch her die.

Laura was in her hospital bed, multiple tubes and wires running from the machines beside her. She was already gone when I entered the room. I held her lifeless body and cried. In my dream I cried for days, never wanting to let her go.

I hadn't seen Laura, or spoken to her ashes, in a long time. I'd tried hard to move on without her. I'd let her memory hold me down for so long. I couldn't save her. I couldn't bring her back. When I lost Joy, I took a different approach. I put her death out of mind and tried to forget about her. I'd done a pretty good job, until that dream. I hadn't kept her safe. It was a warning. Both dreams were a warning. People close to you die. I was about to involve my friends in a potentially dangerous enterprise. I wasn't keeping them safe.

I woke up with a disturbed feeling. I remembered every aspect of my dreams. Omens like that are not to be trifled with. I called a team meeting.

"I had some bad dreams last night," I told them. "I was being warned about the dangers ahead. I want the both of you to be aware of the bad omen that I perceive. Someone could get hurt. I don't want either of you to get hurt. There's no shame in all of us just packing it up and moving on. We can just forget all of this and sail away."

"Fuck that bitch," Holly jeered. "She's caused the two of you enough trouble to last a lifetime. Off with her scalp, I say."

"Do I sense a bit of jealousy there?" I asked.

"Maybe a little," she admitted.

"Fair enough," I said. "Jimi?"

"I've been a coward my entire life," he said. "It's time for me to take a stand. I've got enough money to run and hide, but I think we need to settle this once and for all."

"Whatever we decide to do," I said. "However we handle this, your personal safety is first and foremost. Understood?"

"We've got your back, Breeze," Holly said.

"Yea, we're in," Jimi said. "Danger be damned."

Nineteen

We traded ideas all morning. It was Jimi who first suggested baiting her.

"You've got the State's Attorney on your side," he said. "He baited her once with the bribe. Now we use me for bait. She won't be able to resist."

"What are you suggesting, exactly?" I asked.

"I go out in the open, walk around, let her find me," he said.

"Then when she tries to take you out, the cops pounce?"

"Something like that," he said. "I haven't worked out the details."

"It's got some holes in it," I said. "She'll have someone else do her dirty work. We might not even be able to tie her to it."

"Plus it sounds dangerous," Holly said. "We're supposed to be limiting our exposure to danger."

"We need to make sure it's Taylor herself who tries something," I said. "For that we need me as bait."

"Why you?" asked Jimi.

"I think she's probably madder at me right now than you," I said. "I've embarrassed her."

"She wants to rip your heart out and eat it," said Holly.

"You should have seen her in that interrogation room," I said. "That's about how she acted."

"So if you set up a meeting with her, she won't be able to resist," said Jimi. "She'll bring a gun, maybe."

"Or poison," said Holly. "Women prefer poison to guns."

"I appreciate your feminine perspective," I said. "But what pretext do I have to want to meet with her? What if she just pops a cap in my ass?"

It was obvious that our plan needed more thought. We retired to the pool to give our brains a rest. After a dip in the water and a few cold beers, the situation seemed less urgent. Taylor was royally screwed. We'd gotten her busted. Her career was finished. My personal vengeance might go unfulfilled, but I'd won. I was about to suggest a permanent vacation to my friends when Jimi's phone rang. After answering it, he handed it to me.

"It's Russell," he said.

"What's up?" I answered. "Did you find some legal basis for moving on Taylor?"

"Worse," he said.

"What do you have?" I asked.

"What I have is a dead body," he said.

"Who is it?"

"It's not who he is that's important," he said. "It's what he is, or was."

"Fill me in," I said.

"Our victim was a financial planner down here in Fort Myers," he said.

"Victim plus body equals murder," I surmised.

"Single gunshot to the chest," he said. "The guy hung on long enough for the paramedics

250

to arrive. Said two words with his final breath."

"Am I supposed to guess?"

"Taylor Ford," he said. "The guy whispered the words Taylor Ford to the paramedic on scene."

"Taylor killing a finance guy can only mean one thing," I said. "She's pulled the same scam that she pulled with Jimi, except this time she's got the money and the patsy is dead."

"Doesn't take a genius to figure out," he said. "We sent officers to her home and office right away, but we didn't find her. There's a BOLO for the entire state of Florida."

"She's in the wind," I said.

"Her car will turn up somewhere," he said. "Probably an airport. In the meantime I've requested warrants for both addresses."

"What are we looking for?" I asked.

"We?"

"Oh, come on, Russell," I said. "You called me. I can help. I know her."

"What would you look for?" he asked.

"Straight to her computers," I said. "Emails, who she has been corresponding with. Airline reservations. Car rentals. Hotels. Money transfers. Jimi can have all that stuff in minutes. He knows her too."

"I can't just let you two loose with her data," he said. "The FBI guy will have to do it."

"FBI?"

"We've got a murder," he said. "Now we have a fugitive who will most likely cross state lines and most probably leave the country."

"So she runs to a country with no extradition treaty," I said. "Look for that search on her computers too."

"If she does that we won't be able to get to her," he said.

"I will," I replied. "I will."

"Look, I will not condone any interference by civilians," he said. "I just wanted to make you aware of the circumstances."

"And pick my brain while you're at it," I said.

"Well, yes," he said. "But I'm not asking you to find her. Leave that to the FBI."

"This all happened pretty soon after you let her go," I said. "She's been siphoning money off her clients for some time now, obviously, but maybe she rushed into shooting her accomplice. Maybe she made some mistakes. Get her computers. Let me know what you find."

"Listen, Breeze," he said. "If by some chance she comes after you or Jimi, or if you hear from her, I need to know about it. Do not take matters into your own hands."

"I'm guessing she's already out of the country," I said. "But we will protect ourselves until you figure out where she went."

"I'll call you when we have something," he said.

I handed the phone back to Jimi. He looked a little shaken. The dead guy could have been him.

"Don't sweat it," I said. "Your gut told you something was wrong. You took action. That's why you're still alive."

"I don't think I'm cut out for this," he said. "I didn't imagine that she could kill."

"Me neither, bud," I said. "She fooled us both."

"What do we do now," asked Holly.

"The FBI will find something," I said. "Russell will tell me. Then I go after her."

"We're still a team," she said. "Unless Jimi is too chicken, but I'm still in."

We both turned to look at Jimi. The news that Taylor had killed the financial planner had really spooked him. He'd been in line to catch a bullet, without knowing it. He'd been lucky to dodge a similar fate. Of course, if she had succeeded in killing Jimi, this other guy would still be alive. She'd have gotten her money and ran a long time ago. I wouldn't blame him for sitting this one out.

"I feel responsible," he said. "I also feel dumb that she played me so well. I think I'd like to help. Just try not to put me in front of any bullets."

"I warned you both about the dangers," I reminded them. "That was before she shot someone. It could be one of us next time."

"Or she could be the one getting shot," Holly said.

"Do you think you could really shoot her?" I asked. "Or anyone?"

"If it comes to that," she said. "I guess we'll find out."

"Let's all meet at my boat," I said. "Bring whatever weapons and ammo you have. We'll take inventory and start getting ready to move."

Holly brought a sleek and oiled nine millimeter. She had a box of two hundred and fifty rounds. Jimi had a rusty .357 with one extra clip. My personal weapon of choice was a shotgun. I'd been forced to use it more than once. It had served me well. It wasn't something that you could carry around town though, so I had a nine millimeter as well. Between Holly and I we had over five hundred rounds.

Holly went back to her boat briefly, returning with a cleaning kit and some tools. She started breaking down Jimi's pistol and cleaning it. She obviously knew what she was doing.

"Done much shooting?" I asked her.

"I go to the range when I can," she said. "I plink bottles and stuff when I'm offshore."

"How about you Jimi?" I asked.

"I shot it six times when I bought it," he said. "Hasn't been fired since."

"Did you hit the target?" I asked.

"Almost," he said. "Guess I'm not much of a gun guy."

We had our little arsenal. Holly could shoot. Jimi couldn't. I was comfortable with the shotgun, but hadn't fired my own pistol in years. I was a decent shot back then, but no sharpshooter. What were we supposed to do with our firepower? I wasn't sure. We'd find Taylor and bring her to justice, one way or another. We knew that she was armed, unless she'd had someone else pull the trigger. If that was the case, the dead man had known who ordered the hit.

We went through checklists for our boats. We didn't need all three, or even two. Holly was the most prepared to leave. She'd been ready to leave at a moment's notice for days. If a boat was to be part of our chase, we'd use *Another Adventure*.

Russell called back the next day. Taylor's car had been found at the airport in Fort Myers.

She'd booked a flight to Nassau. Gate agents recalled her boarding the plane.

"Sloppy," said Russell. "She left a clear trail."

"What's our extradition agreement with the Bahamas?" I asked.

"We have a treaty," he answered. "They'll send her back if they find her. Problem is they don't look real hard. They've got limited resources."

"Can the FBI go over there?"

"The FBI does not generally conduct law enforcement outside the United States," he said.

"You sound like you're reading from the Code of Federal Regulations," I said.

"They have to work with authorities in the other country," he explained. "They can't make an arrest without an act of Congress."

"What about her computers?" I asked. "Has she searched any specific places in the Bahamas?"

"Still working on that," he said. "She deleted her history, but the tech guy says he can recover it."

"Emails?"

"Does the name Frederick C. Ford mean anything to you?" he asked. "President of Airglades International Airport. President and CEO at Florida Cargo Fresh."

"Captain Fred," I said. "No relation to Taylor."

"You know him?" he asked. "She's been corresponding with him."

"He's the guy I told you to stay away from," I said. "The power broker that helped me bribe a judge. I introduced him to Taylor."

"Is he in the Bahamas?" he asked.

"Last I knew he was in Georgetown," I said. "I just left there not too long ago."

"So Taylor is going to Georgetown," he said.

"I don't know," I said. "Seems too simple. It can't be that easy."

"You think she's sending us on a wild goose chase?"

"Like I said, she was in a hurry," I said. "Maybe she made mistakes."

"It's all we've got so far," he said.

"Captain Fred lives on a big yacht," I told him. "Wouldn't be a problem to move to another island, or even another country. Where would she be safe from extradition?"

"Bermuda comes to mind," he said. "Any number of Caribbean countries."

"So my working theory is that she hooks up with Captain Fred, and they boogie out of the Bahamas to one of those places that won't ship her back to the US."

"She lives happily ever after with her stolen money, and she adds Fred's money to it," he said.

"If Captain Fred knew what she was up to," I said. "He wouldn't be a party to it."

"Incredibly sexy women have been known to persuade older men with money," he said.

"Younger ones too," I said. "She does have certain powers."

"We'll keep working with her computers," he said. "See if we can pin down an ultimate destination."

"I'll be assembling my team and preparing to depart for the Bahamas," I said. "Call me immediately if you get anything useful. After I get over there, communication will get difficult."

"This is where I lecture you not to do this," he said.

"Save your breath," I said.

"I figured as much," he said. "One last thing. The gun was a .38, most likely an old police revolver."

"How would you know that?" I asked.

"Local departments all switched to Glocks a few years back," he said. "The old revolvers were sold at auction. That's where Taylor bought hers. It's duly registered."

As soon as I hung up, I felt the old familiar feelings begin to stir. The chase always got my blood pumping. People ran. I hunted them down. Sometimes I ran, and people hunted me. Such was the life of Breeze. My friends and I had been feeling the itch to move on for days. We'd been sitting still for too long. Now we all had a purpose. One thing was different this time. I wasn't alone. There was three of us. Holly and Jimi had committed to this. I needed to devise a plan that would take advantage of the extra help, but keep them out of harm's way if at all possible. Holly had proven to be more than capable. Jimi was dead weight. I decided to talk it over with

Holly. Hopefully, she'd have some ideas. I knew that we needed to move fast. I had to get to Georgetown in a hurry. Sailing *Another Adventure* just wasn't fast enough.

Twenty

Leap of Faith wouldn't get me there fast enough either. I needed to fly to Georgetown, but if Captain Fred took off in his boat, I'd need a boat to follow him. That is, if Taylor even hooked up with Fred in Georgetown. I had my reservations about the entire mission. Taylor was smart. Fred was smart too. I wanted to keep my friends out of danger. I decided that I'd fly down alone. Holly and Jimi could bring her boat down after me. I'd either settle the matter as soon as I hit the ground, or I'd have a boat and partners to continue the pursuit. It was all I could come up with. There was no time to waste.

Holly was hesitant at first. She wanted to be there if I confronted Taylor in Georgetown. I convinced her that having a boat available if she wasn't there was crucial. If we all flew down there together to find that her and

Captain Fred had left on his boat, we'd be stuck with no way to track them down.

"I can take the southern route across the Cay Sal Bank," said Holly. "We'll sail south of Andros and over to the southern Exumas. If Jimi is any help at all, we can make it in three days from the Keys."

"He should be able to stand watch while you sleep," I said. "You'll need good weather and wind to make it that fast."

"How will we get in touch with you once we arrive?" she asked.

"I could take the handheld VHF," I proposed.

"Only good for five miles tops," she countered. "You really need to get a phone."

"Everyone keeps telling me that," I said. "Can I just use Jimi's phone?"

"We need SIM cards for the Bahamas," she said.

"Have them overnighted to the marina," I said. "We hit the road tomorrow."

We walked over to Jimi's boat to bring him up to speed. He had an overnight bag packed. I had him make me a flight reservation for the next afternoon. I'd be in Georgetown by nightfall.

"You're going to be a hardcore sailor for the next four days or so," I told Jimi. "Do what Holly tells you. Don't fall asleep on watch. Rest when you're not at the helm. I'll need you both awake and alert when you get there."

"What if you already find her before we get there?" he asked.

"Then you've had a nice long sail for nothing," I replied. "But you'll be in Paradise."

"What if she's not there at all?" asked Holly.

"I'll poke around town while I'm waiting for you," I told her. "She's a very recognizable woman. If she's been around someone will remember her. I'd drum up a lead somehow."

"Because it's what you do," she said.

"I'm familiar with Georgetown," I said. "I've been there enough to know some people."

"It's a big ocean out there, Breeze," she said. "It's going to be tough if they've split town."

"It'll work out," I said. "We'll find them."

"I wish I had your confidence," she said.

"Right now, just worry about getting you and your boat there in one piece," I said.

"Aye, aye, captain," she said.

We each made our final preparations for our respective trips. I couldn't smuggle a pistol on the plane, which was troublesome. I'd be unarmed until Holly and Jimi arrived. I wondered if I could pick up a new piece on the street in Georgetown. They weren't big on gun ownership in the Bahamas, although it was okay to bring them into the country on a boat. You were supposed to declare them when you checked in with Customs. We weren't sure if Holly would be checking in at all on this trip. We were facing multiple unknowns. Any carefully made plan would be certain to fall apart. That's why I didn't have one. I was just going to show up and see what happened. It's how I worked. I adapted. I made the best of whatever situation presented itself. Other people call that winging it. I call it being prepared for any eventuality. I tried to think fast. I let instinct and reflex guide me when the shit hit the fan.

We all met at Leverock's Restaurant for dinner. I picked up the tab for all of us. We made small talk. We didn't discuss our mission in public. Jimi excused himself after finishing his meal. Holly and I walked back to the marina together. As we neared my slip, I took her hand and tugged her towards my boat. She stopped and gave me a questioning look. I nodded yes. We agreed to make love without saying a word.

We kept if soft, gentle and slow. We shared each other like real lovers do. We had developed the sort of friendship where neither of us spoke of it as anything more. We'd stopped analyzing love and the meaning of life. We just enjoyed each other when we could, knowing full well that either of us could be gone at a moment's notice. Somehow, we'd come to terms with that without ever mentioning it. When it was over, she got up and started to dress.

"You can stay," I told her, wanting her to be with me for the night.

"I want to," she said. "But I've got charts to go over. I need time with my boat to prepare mentally."

"I understand," I said.

"Good night, Breeze."

"Good night, Holly."

The after-effects of lovemaking allowed me to sleep deeply. I had no disturbing dreams. No little angels or devils appeared to advise me. No dead lovers haunted me. My mind was clear. It was all about the mission.

I was up before the dawn. So was Holly. We rousted Jimi and the two of them tossed the lines as soon as our SIM cards arrived. I took Jimi's car to the airport. I had to change planes in Fort Lauderdale to get a direct flight into Georgetown. There was a delay. I didn't land until after dark. I had trouble getting a cab into town. I had trouble getting a room. Downtown Georgetown doesn't have much to offer the traveler seeking a hotel room. I finally ended up at the Peace and Plenty. It was much too late to get a boat to look for Captain Fred.

I felt lost without my boat. I had trouble sleeping in a real bed, on land. I wished there had been a way to include *Miss Leap* in this deal, but *Another Adventure* was bigger and faster than my slow trawler. Neither Taylor nor Fred knew what Holly's boat looked like. That might be to our advantage. We could get close without them knowing. I knew Fred's boat quite well. I'd been on it many times. It was big and easily identifiable. There weren't many places to hide a seventy foot Hatteras.

Incognito was fairly fast for its size, but it burned an incredible amount of fuel. He'd have to make frequent stops if he ran. There weren't that many places to buy fuel between there and Nassau. If I had to track him, he'd leave a trail of information, assuming the locals were willing to talk to me.

I had a few beers at the hotel bar and turned in for the night. In the morning, I walked through town until I got to Redboone's Café. Redboone's was at the top of the dinghy dock and was the central meeting place for cruisers. I called Elvis, the water taxi driver. He said he'd pick me up at ten. I ordered a breakfast sandwich while I waited. I washed it down with a cold Kalik, even though it was still early in the morning. Land taxi drivers hung around looking for fares. A few cruisers swapped stories from their travels. An old man in a battered pickup set up his produce stand. His first order of business was to put up his umbrella to block the sun.

No one in attendance cared about murders or stolen money. They knew nothing of beautiful women on fancy yachts. I fit in there. They were boat bums like me, or poor locals just trying to survive. The cruisers came here to escape. The blue water and white sand beaches were the main draw. On land, they found soul crushing poverty like they'd never seen back home. Mostly, they came to town for groceries and returned to the harbor without delay. Hanging around town gave the more industrious locals a chance to figure out how they could make some money off of you.

I was looking for a certain type of local. I didn't need the guy peddling weed. I certainly didn't need the guy bumming cigarettes. The head taxi man looked official, not the kind of man to ask about a gun. The bartender was just a kid. I didn't see anyone that I felt comfortable asking about acquiring a weapon. I finished my breakfast and walked down to the dinghy dock. Elvis was early. I hopped on board his boat.

"Where to?" he asked.

"Redshanks," I told him. "The big Hatteras, Incognito."

"It's not there, man," he said.

"It's gone?"

"Left yesterday," he said.

"You know the boat?" I asked. "Do you know Captain Fred?"

"Everybody knows the boat," he said. "He brought it up here to the Exuma Yacht Club a few days ago. He had a bunch of food delivered. Filled up with fuel. Everybody see he's going on a trip. He sit back there in Redshanks for years. All of the sudden he move on."

"Do you know where he was going?" I asked.

"No, man," he answered. "But he went out that way, like he was heading north."

"Passengers?" I asked. I was hoping Elvis had seen Taylor.

"I didn't see nobody," he said. "Just the old man."

"Have you seen a smoking hot redhead around lately?" I asked.

"I'd remember that for sure," he said. "No pretty redheads been on board. No sir."

I was a day late. Yesterday, Fred had been right there in town. I couldn't have missed him. Now he was gone. There was no sign of

Taylor yet, either. I asked Elvis to take me over to the Saint Francis Resort. Taylor and I had stayed there during our visit with Captain Fred previously. It was a long shot, but I had to start somewhere. I had a few days before Holly and Jimi would show up. I got a room at Saint Francis and looked around.

I checked the dining room at lunch and dinner. No Taylor. I checked the beach. No Taylor. I asked a few tourists about her. No luck. There were no desk clerks like at American hotels. The owners took care of everything. They knew you were coming, because you had to arrive by boat. They hadn't seen a pretty redhead either.

I got Elvis to take me to the Chat N Chill the next day. I sat and drank Kaliks all day long. No pretty redheads were seen. On the third day, Elvis took me back to town. I sat and talked with the cab drivers. About midday, my old friend Clifford the cab driver showed up. He remembered me.

"Did you find the dreadlock dude?" he asked. "That was one ugly little fellow."

"I found him," I said. "Way up in the Everglades he was. Tough little shit, but I got him."

"Welcome back to our island," he said. "You looking for somebody else or just enjoying paradise?"

"I'm looking for a very beautiful lady," I said.

"Aren't we all?" he said, laughing.

"This one has flowing auburn hair," I said. "She's a stunner."

"Yup," he said. "I gave this lady a ride from the airport the other day."

"She's here?" I asked.

"No, not here," he said. "I took her up north to Emerald Bay. There's a Sandals resort up there. That's where I dropped her."

"When was this?"

"Not yesterday," he said. "Day before, I think."

I gave Clifford a twenty for his troubles.

"Thanks, Mr. Breeze," he said. "Anytime, you hear?"

I turned on Jimi's phone and tried to figure out how to access the internet. Redboone's had free wifi. I had to ask for the password. A lady sailor twenty years my elder showed me how to log in. It took a few different Google searches, but I found it. Sandals Emerald Bay billed itself as exquisite sophistication in the exotic Bahamian out islands. It had villas and suites and seven restaurants along a one mile stretch of beach. It also had a marina. Captain Fred was on his way to meet Taylor at Emerald Bay. That had to be it.

Things were falling into place. I'd taken the information that was available and added it to what I learned since arriving. I could put my finger on a map and show you where she was. I didn't have her, but I was closing in. I desperately wanted to go after her, but Holly and Jimi were due at any time. I was unarmed until they arrived.

I bought another Kalik at Redboone's. Cold beer helped me to think. Holly wouldn't have a cell signal until she was almost to Georgetown. At first I thought there was no point in trying to call her. It dawned on me that I could leave her a message. As soon as she got within range, she'd see that I had called.

"I know where she is," I said. "Get here fast. I'm in town at Redboone's. I'll be at Saint Francis tonight. Don't mess around. Come get me as soon as you get your anchor down."

There was nothing else to do but wait. More Kalik's helped pass the time.

Twenty-One

Holly called back late that afternoon. They were less than an hour out. I badly wanted to jump aboard and immediately head north towards Emerald Bay. Holly's voice betrayed her fatigue. I soon gathered that things hadn't gone well during their trip.

"You two okay?" I asked. "How soon can you travel? We're on her tail."

"We are not," Holly said. "We're both exhausted. We've been pounding into heavy seas for two days. We had to tack to hell and back to get across from Andros. Everything is soaked. No way we can continue tonight. We have to get some rest."

"I was afraid of that," I said. "Sorry to hear you've had a rough time of it."

"We got here as fast as humanly possible," she said. "But we're paying the price."

"Is the boat okay?" I asked.

"She can take more than we can," she replied. "Just need to dry her out some."

"I've got a room," I said. "You two should sleep there. Can you pick me up at the dinghy dock once you get anchored?"

"A hot shower would help," she said. "I'll call you back when the anchor is down."

I was disappointed. I guessed that Jimi wasn't enough help to allow Holly to get any sleep. Another day slipped away from us. If Captain Fred got too far ahead, we'd never find him. I ordered another Kalik and cursed Taylor under my breath. Three more beers went down before Holly called again.

"I'm on my way to get you," she said. "I'm leaving Jimi here to pull some of the cushions and straighten up a bit. We'll pick him up on the way back."

"Great," I'll be ready."

On the dinghy ride back, Holly gave me a rundown of the past few days. They'd been fine and made good time until they cleared the southern end of Andros. The winds turned east and seas got sloppy. Jimi could stand watch, but he couldn't turn the boat when it came time to tack. He woke her every hour so she could help swing around and reset the autopilot. She never had enough time to really sleep deeply.

He'd also left the companionway door open when he went out on deck. Waves washed over the rail and saltwater ran down inside the salon. Earlier, Holly had been instructing Jimi on safe gun handling and shooting. They'd left the pistols on the salon table. They ended up on the floor and under water. Holly had spent hours disassembling and cleaning them. Jimi's rusty weapon wouldn't cooperate. The spring for the hammer was badly corroded. It failed to fire half the time. We were down to two handguns.

Holly looked like hell. She had dark circles and a darker frown. Jimi looked beat as well. Long hard days at sea in rough weather will do that to even seasoned sailors. Jimi was a novice. He didn't like it much. We all went back to my room at Saint Francis. They each got a shower and then we shared a hot meal. The room had one king-sized bed and a couch. Jimi graciously volunteered to take the couch. Holly and I slept together, without touching at all. We didn't even share a goodnight kiss. She was out and snoring within minutes. Jimi sang his own sleepy song across the room.

I'd expected too much from my friends. Somewhere out there in the night, Taylor was drinking champagne and counting her money. We were in no shape to go after her.

I woke up first. Both of my friends were still out of it. I let them sleep. I went downstairs to get breakfast. I paced the grounds, looking out to sea. At that point, I could only hope that Captain Fred was in no hurry. He had filled up with fuel before he left Georgetown. If he decided to put the throttles down and cruise hard, all hope was lost. At nine, I returned to the room to find Holly awake and Jimi stirring. Holly was coming out of the bathroom, wiping her face with a towel. Her white girl dreads were a little more tangled than usual. She never wore makeup, but she didn't need it. Her dark circles were gone. She gave me a smile.

"Morning, Breeze," she said. "We should already be underway."

"You needed your beauty sleep," I told her. "Him too."

"No amount of beauty sleep is going to make him pretty," she said, laughing.

"I heard that," said Jimi.

"It's alive," I said.

"Just barely," Jimi replied. "I don't think I'm cut out for blue water sailing. That shit was brutal."

"At least you didn't get sick," said Holly. "That's something."

"Do you two think you're ready to go?" I asked.

They both said they were good to go. The trip to Emerald Bay was a short one. If Fred was gone, we'd regroup there. If they needed more rest, they'd get it. If worse came to worse, I'd pilot *Another Adventure* myself for a few hours so they could sleep. They got a quick breakfast before we headed out in the dinghy. The sun shone overhead. The sky was as blue as the water. A moderate breeze came in from the east. It was a fine day to apprehend a murderer.

The anchor went up at the same time as the sails. Holly laid us off the wind and turned towards the northern exit of Elizabeth Harbor. She fiddled with a few winches until she was happy. The high hills blocked some of the wind. We slowly weaved through the other anchored boats until we cleared the last of the hills. The ocean breeze heeled us over as we gained speed. In spite of it all, Holly smiled. She really did love to be at the wheel of *Another Adventure* with the wind in her sails. Her smile was infectious. Jimi and I smiled back.

"So what exactly are we supposed to do when we find her," asked Jimi.

"We take her into custody and call the FBI," I said. "She's a known fugitive, a suspect in a murder. They'll come get her."

"We just nab her and hold her," said Holly. "You make it sound so simple."

"What's the problem?" I asked. "Simple is good."

"She's armed, for starters," Holly said. "We don't know where Fred stands. Maybe he's armed too."

"I don't believe he'll shoot at us," I said. "We're friends. He'll listen to reason, but it would be nice to grab her when she's off his boat. If we can, just to keep him out of it."

"So we grab her," she said. "Then we have to hold her prisoner for a few days. Not so simple."

"There's three of us," I said. "We can do it. She's a petite girly girl for crying out loud."

"And I'm the only one on this boat that hasn't slept with her," she said.

"What's that got to do with anything?" I asked.

"I don't know," she said. "Things could get complicated."

"She can't sweet talk her way out of a murder rap," I said. "Don't over think it. Let's just get it done."

The weather stayed nice. We sailed up the Exuma Sound at a brisk pace. The tall buildings that made up the resort came into view. The entrance was narrow so we couldn't see inside the marina. Holly started the engine while Jimi and I lowered the sails. Our plan that day was a bold one. We'd just motor right in and take a slip. If *Incognito* was there, they didn't know Holly's boat. I'd stay out of sight until we got tied up. Then we'd make a move.

We crawled through the narrow entrance channel with anticipation. Holly got our slip assignment. We cleared the break wall and the entire basin came in to full view. There was no seventy foot Hatteras to be found. Fred and Taylor were gone.

"Now what?" Holly asked.

"We ask around," I said. "See what we can find out."

"You ask around," she said. "I'm taking a nap."

"Me too," Jimi said.

Clearly, my crew was in no hurry to resume the chase.

I made my way up the docks to the marina office. As I paid the bill, I casually asked about *Incognito*. The dock master had no interest in discussing the comings and goings of his customers. I wondered if Fred had paid him to keep quiet. The dockhands were easier. A twenty dollar bill was all it took to get one of them to talk. Yes, a big Hatteras by that name had been here. No, he did not take on fuel. Yes, there was a pretty redhead at the resort. Did she get on the boat? Not sure, but she's gone now. The Hatteras named *Incognito* left yesterday. It went north.

Logical deduction told me that Taylor was now onboard with Fred. They didn't get fuel because the run from Georgetown to Emerald Bay was a short one. He would most likely get fuel at his next stop. Would he hang around long enough for us to catch up? I went back to the boat and pulled out Holly's dog-eared charts. There were a few scattered marinas along the way, but all of them would be difficult to get into with a boat the size of *Incognito*. The next reasonable fuel stop was at Staniel Cay. It had deep water and plenty of room. It also had a nasty current that ran right through the fuel dock. Prudent captains waited for slack tide to approach it. There was a slim chance that we could catch him while he waited at anchor for such an opportunity, but only if we untied the lines and left immediately.

My crew balked. There was no way we were leaving already. They begged for one more night of rest, good food and relaxation. They outnumbered me two to one. I agreed to wait until morning. I didn't like it, but I needed them to be at the top of their game when we confronted Taylor. I let them rest. Later, I treated them to dinner at the resort. We moved to the bar after finishing our meals. Jimi grumbled a bit about the way things were going.

"Feels like we're chasing a ghost," he said. "I'm living on a soggy sailboat, getting beat all to hell for nothing."

"There's an airport right here on this island," I said. "Flights every day to Key West."

"I can't quit now," he said. "I owe you."

"You don't owe me a thing," I said. "You paid me not to give you up."

"It's more than that now," he said. "We're friends. We have Taylor in common. I need to help you if I can."

"You're just not enjoying the ride?" I asked.

"Not really," he admitted. "Living on a sailboat was a lot easier sitting in a marina. It's much tougher out here. The travel is killing me."

"It's not for everyone," Holly said. "Sitting still at a marina kills me."

"Let's keep our focus," I interrupted. "They left here yesterday. I'm guessing they went to Staniel. Maybe they left there today, maybe not. At least we know they are going north. Not many alternatives until they get to Nassau. I'd like to catch them before then."

"What if we don't, and they don't go to Nassau?" asked Holly.

"Everybody goes to Nassau," I said. "Remember, he's got Taylor with him. She won't want to stay at anchor every night. She'll want to go out to eat or go shopping or something. He'll want to pick up some good cigars. They'll stop there, but it will be hard to get close to them in the city. Much better to confront them out in the islands."

"So we run hard and catch up to the fuckers," Holly said.

"If you two are up to it," I said.

"Okay, okay," said Jimi. "Let me sleep tonight and then we bust ass. Let's get this over with."

"Atta boy," I said.

"All for one and shit," said Holly.

We'd had a little rough patch, but the team was one again. All of us were up early in the morning, ready to go. We untied from the dock and eased out of the marina before first light. Holly had the sails up before we got past the break wall. As soon as the wind caught them, she killed the engine. We glided through the soft rollers like a Viking ship, seeking battle. We had eight hours to go before we'd find out if the battle would happen. If not, the chase would continue. *You can run, Taylor, but you can't hide.*

We chose Farmer's Cut to cross back to the inside. The current was strong but the seas were calm. It slowed us down dramatically, but only for a short time. Traveling on the Banks instead of the Sound would be much more comfortable. We headed north towards Staniel Cay. I fiddled with Jimi's gun, but it was hopeless. It couldn't be counted on if it was needed. I decided that I would go in unarmed. My friend's safety, and ability to defend themselves, weighed heavily on my mind. They would each carry a pistol.

Traveling up the Exuma Banks does not offer a clear view of the boats docked at Staniel Cay. We'd have to turn off and steer east towards the Thunderball Grotto to get a look. We cruised through the anchorage at Big Majors first. Several yachts rested at anchor there, but not *Incognito*. Holly was worried about making a U-turn in the current off Staniels fuel dock. I reassured her that she was the best captain I knew, at least on a sailboat. She could handle it. We had the current pushing us as we angled closer to get a better look. It carried us by the marina at an alarming speed. We didn't see Captain Fred's boat. I really wanted to stop and ask if he'd been there, but we couldn't anchor in that raging current.

Holly fought the wheel while trying to turn around. When we got sideways to the current, it pushed us seemingly out of control. We were carried on to the east, traveling sideways for more than a hundred yards. Holly throttled up hard, laid the wheel over, and slowly got the bow around and into the flow. We crawled back out of there at three knots, fighting the current all the way. Once back on the Banks, she was able to pull back on the throttle and relax. Where was Fred, and Taylor?

I took a quick glance at the charts and realized I'd overlooked another possibility. HIghborne Cay was fifty miles to the north. It was an exclusive resort marina that didn't welcome trawler trash like me. Maybe that's why I'd put it out of my mind. It catered to larger yachts and wealthy clientele. Taylor and Fred would be more than welcome. It also had a fuel dock that was easily accessible by big boats like Fred's.

We'd already traveled for eight hours. I wanted to push on. We wouldn't make it before running out of daylight, but we might close the gap between us and Fred. We might even find them there. I asked the crew if they were up to continuing on. I got shrugs. They weren't excited by the idea, but they went along. We headed north again at seven knots. I took the wheel so Holly could rest. After a few hours, Jimi took over for me. I went below just as Holly was waking up. We sat in the salon, letting Jimi earn his keep for a change.

"I've been wondering something," Holly said.

"Shoot," I replied.

"What happens when this is all over?" she asked. "Whether we find her or not, what next for us?"

"We've been through this before," I reminded her. "Both of us thought it better to move on."

"I thought so at the time," she said. "Now, I'm not so sure."

"I apologize, but I haven't really thought about it," I admitted. "I've been focused on the job at hand. Tunnel vision."

"I know," she said. "I can see it in your eyes. A man on a mission."

"It's no life for a girl like you," I told her. "You deserve more."

"I'm not sure cleaning boat bottoms for a living is more," she said. "I'll have to work to survive. I'll be poor and boring."

"Boring is good sometimes," I said. "Much safer than this."

"I don't know if I can handle it," she said. "Plus, I'd really miss you. I missed you when we split the last time."

"Until you latched on to a young buck," I said, laughing. "Go find another one. You'll forget all about old Breeze."

"Not likely," she said. "You and I, we're not husband and wife, and I guess we never will be, but there's something special between us. Admit it."

"I can't deny the truth," I said. "I just don't know where that leaves us."

"Think about coming to the Keys when this is over," she said. "Please?"

"Marathon?" I asked.

"You'll find me," she said. "It's what you do."

Darkness set in. We stayed on course. We let Jimi go below to get some sleep. The wind had completely died so we were motoring. Holly hated motoring, plus we were burning fuel. There was nothing we could do about it though. We motored on into the night. It was well after midnight when we made our approach to the anchorage off Highborne Cay. Mega-yachts dotted the skyline. A few cruising boats had chosen the northern part of the anchorage. It was an area of good holding just off a nice beach. We headed towards them.

In the gap between the huge yachts and the smaller cruising boats, a seventy foot Hatteras swung on her anchor. *Incognito* was in the harbor. We'd found Taylor and Fred. We slid on by and nestled ourselves in with the smaller boats. It was almost two in the morning when we got settled on our anchor. It looked like everyone was asleep on the other boats. We decided to do the same. We'd been on the move for over fifteen hours. Even though we'd taken turns resting, enough was enough. We'd have our showdown soon enough.

Twenty-Two

For more than one reason, I couldn't sleep. I didn't really know what I wanted as far as a future with Holly was concerned. I didn't think she knew what she wanted either. I was too old for her. I had zero stability in life. I wasn't a part of normal society. I generally stayed off the grid, with no purpose other than to live day by day. I had no future. I tried to tell myself that I wanted more for her. She didn't need to waste her life with the likes of me. When it got right down to it, though, I like having her around. Saying goodbye would difficult. I'd miss her terribly.

Then there was Taylor. I'd burned her ass with the bribery sting. She'd gone off the deep end and shot someone for money. She thought she'd gotten away. I sat just a few hundred yards away from her at that moment. She'd be beaten once and for all when I grabbed her. I would win. She'd be brought to justice and I'd disappear, like I always did. It was a lot for a simple boat bum to take in.

I faced the morning with a burning desire to finish my mission. Taylor's day of reckoning was at hand. I watched *Incognito* through binoculars. I tried to stay calm. I had to keep my cool. I saw Captain Fred serve Taylor breakfast on the upper after-deck. They both wore fancy robes. He chewed on a stubby cigar. She drank from a champagne flute, probably a mimosa. Life was good.

I watched as they boarded his tender. She carried a beach bag in one hand and a book in the other. My eyes followed them to the beach. Fred helped her out of the tender and walked her up the beach to a waiting gazebo. They talked for a minute as she got settled in the shade. Fred got back into the tender and headed back to his boat. She was alone on the beach. This was it. I gathered my team to strategize. There was a trail that left the marina and went up over a hill. It led to the same gazebo. We'd take the dinghy around to the other side, climb the hill, and descend upon her. Holly and Jimi would branch off to flank her. I'd come directly down the trail.

Her back would be to me, as she sat facing the beach. My friends carried the pistols. I was unarmed.

We stopped just before cresting the hill. I looked them both in the eye and nodded. They both nodded back. We were ready.

"Stay concealed as best you can," I told them. "She may have her weapon. She will recognize you both. Wait until the last minute."

Holly split off to my right. The beach grass and brush was waist high. Jimi moved to the left, half crawling through the sea grapes and shrubbery. Slowly and quietly, I went down the path towards Taylor. I gave my team time to get into position. Finally, I walked right on out to the beach, behind the gazebo.

Taylor had her nose in a book. I didn't think she sensed my approach. I was wrong.

"Hi Taylor," I said. "Fancy meeting you here."

She was standing and facing me in a split second. Her hair spun with her as she turned, framing her lovely face like it always did. She was wearing a barely there red bikini. It contrasted nicely with her porcelain skin.

Everything about her screamed beauty, except the gun she held in her right hand. It was an old police revolver.

"You shouldn't have come after me," she said.

"You knew that I would," I said. "You made it easy."

"You won't be so smart with a hole in your head," she said.

"Come on, Taylor," I said. "You don't want to shoot me. Put the gun down. It's over."

"It's you or me, Breeze," she said. "Sorry."

I watched as she raised the pistol and took careful aim. A dozen calculations ran through my head in an instant. I wasn't completely out of her gun's range, but I was at the far end of its accuracy. I was slightly uphill from her position, adding another variable to her aim. She didn't waver in her stance. Her eyes were cold. She was going to shoot.

She pulled the hammer back. I heard a shot ring out. I flinched, bracing for the impact that would never come. I opened my eyes. I saw Taylor drop to both knees, hover there for a second, and finally fall forward on her face. Bright red liquid oozed from the hole in her back.

Holly came into view from my right. A wisp of smoke still trailed out of the barrel of her pistol. The shot that she'd made was even tougher than the one Taylor never got to try. We both walked towards Taylor's body. Holly was shaking.

"Is she dead?" she asked.

I knelt down for a closer inspection. She was breathing. I felt her neck for a pulse. She was still alive. I yelled for Jimi, but he was already at our side.

"Oh Christ," he said. "What do we do now?"

"What do we do, Breeze?" asked Holly.

"Either, we run and she dies," I said. "Or we get help. I vote help."

"Yea, get help," said Jimi.

"Help her," Holly said.

"Jimi, go back and get the dinghy," I ordered. "Bring it around here to the beach. Hurry."

I took my shirt off and pushed it over the bullet hole. I turned Taylor on her side to check for an exit wound. There was none.

The last time I'd held a bleeding woman in my arms, she'd died. I really didn't want a replay of that. Blood came out of her mouth. It was bright red and foamy, indicating that the shot had gone through a lung.

"She's going to die, isn't she?" said Holly. "Shit. I killed her."

"She's not dead yet," I said. "But it would be me laying here if not for you."

"She was going to shoot you," she said.

"You did good, Holly," I said. "You did what had to be done. Thanks."

"It doesn't feel good," she said. "I think I'm gonna be sick."

Jimi brought the dinghy around and beached it. I had to release the pressure on her wound to pick Taylor up. I instructed Jimi to put his hand on the shirt and push while I cradled her. While we walked down to the dinghy, Holly retched at the edge of the dunes. I sat forward, with Taylor in my lap. Jimi pushed us off and started the outboard. Holly climbed in and we were off.

"Where to?" asked Jimi.

"Take us to Fred's boat," I said. "Drop us off. You two get out of here. Ditch the guns. Run back to Florida and lay low."

"What about you?" Holly asked. "We can't leave you here."

"I'll catch up," I said. "I promise. Just go."

Jimi was good with it. Holly was not.

"Damn you, Breeze," she said. "You and I have unfinished business. I need you right now. I shot her for you."

"I know you did," I said. "But I can't let you get arrested for it. I need you to run."

She started crying. She was still in shock. Things were happening so fast. We were approaching *Incognito*. Taylor was still breathing. I wanted to hold Holly. I wanted to hug her and tell her everything was going to be fine. I wanted to remind her that shit works out, but Taylor prevented me.

"I need you to be strong," I said. "Hold on for a little bit longer. Put that boat of yours in the wind and haul ass out of here. I need you too, Holly. I need you to be free. I'll find you."

We came up behind the stern of Fred's boat. When he first recognized me, he smiled from ear to ear. His expression quickly changed. He saw Taylor. He saw the blood. I didn't know if he would help, or if he would shoot me himself.

"What the fuck have you done?" he screamed.

"No time to explain," I said. "Call for help. Call BASRA. Call someone now."

Captain Fred was a deeply experienced man. He was capable in all things. He'd seen the world, and many of the horrors that it could produce. He dismissed his anger and his fear and took control of the situation. He directed us to a sofa, where we put Taylor down. He sent Jimi after a first-aid kit. He dialed the phone at the same time. I ran Jimi off.

"Get Holly out of here," I told him. "Time to man up, buddy. She needs your help. Go."

Holly was still in the dinghy. She was still crying. She'd shot a human being. That made her cry. She was losing me. That made her cry too. It broke my heart.

Fred had exposed the wound. He sprinkled some kind of powder into it, which almost instantly stopped the bleeding. He cleaned it up and applied a clean bandage. It looked like he'd done it all before.

"Small caliber," he said. "No stopping power. No exit wound. That's the good. The bad is that sometimes they bounce around instead of lodging into bone or going all the way through. More internal damage."

"Nine millimeter," I told him. "From a good distance."

"You've got a lot of explaining to do," he said.

"I didn't shoot her, Fred," I said. "I'm trying to save her."

BASRA sent a helicopter to the island. We took Taylor into the marina with Fred's tender. A golf cart took her to the road where the chopper waited. It was bound for Nassau. The island had one police officer, who came to question me. His breath smelled like booze.

"Where did this happen?" the officer asked.

"On the beach, at the gazebo," I told him.

"Did you see it happen?"

"No. I had walked down the beach. I heard a shot and I came running."

"You ran towards the shot?" he asked.

"Yes," I answered. "It sounded like it came from the gazebo, where Taylor was."

"You were with her?" he asked.

"I'm crew on Fred's vessel," I lied. Fred raised an eyebrow but didn't object.

"So you took the lady to the beach, where someone shot her?"

"I didn't see who did it," I said.

"Was there anyone fleeing the scene?" he asked. "By boat or on foot?"

"Not that I noticed," I said. "I saw a few boats moving around, but they didn't look like they were fleeing. I was more concerned about Taylor. I just didn't think."

He turned to address Fred.

"I'm going to ask you to remain where you are," he said. "I am just a simple constable. Nassau will send a detective to speak with you both."

"I understand," said Fred. "Incognito will remain anchored where she is."

The cop looked at me.

"I've don't have any more information that would help," I said. "I've told you everything I can remember."

"You'll wait for the detective," he said. "I'll summon him now. Should be here tomorrow."

I had no intention of waiting around, but I had to deal with Captain Fred first. I had no method of transportation. *Another Adventure* had set sail immediately. I was happy to see her sails go up, but I was stuck.

"Start talking, Breeze," said Fred. "How did Taylor end up with a bullet in her?"

"She's not what you think she is," I said.

"Right now I think she's a trauma patient," he said. "You had something to do with it."

"She's a prime suspect in a murder," I told him. "I came here to bring her in."

"Since when do you work for law enforcement?" he asked.

"I don't," I said. "It's personal."

"It's personal for me too," he said.

"Don't tell me you were sleeping with her," I said.

"She wanted to go to Bermuda," he said.

"Because they won't extradite her," I told him. "Couldn't you see through her? No offense, but why would she sleep with you?"

"Did you?" he asked. "Did you see through her when she was screwing you?"

"I guess not," I said. "Point taken."

"Maybe you should start from the beginning," he said. "What the hell is going on?"

I told him the whole story. It didn't sound real as I told it. I could hardly believe it myself. Taylor had manipulated wealthy investors, politicians, judges, Jimi, Fred, and myself. Through a series of ruses, bluffs, and bullshit, I'd been able to unravel all of her misdeeds. The job of making her pay had also fallen to me. I'd originally introduced Taylor to Fred. I'd asked him to help her and he had. It was natural for her to return to him when she was in need again. I couldn't blame him for falling for her false charm. He couldn't blame me for hunting her down. We called a truce, and tried to figure out what to do next.

"I need to get out of here," I said. "They don't even know my name. I can just disappear."

"They'll certainly see this boat leaving the harbor," he said.

"What about the tender?" I asked. "Run me down to Staniel. I can catch a plane in the morning."

"What do I tell the detective when he shows up?" he asked.

"You woke up and I was gone," I said.

"They'll want to know who you are," he said. "You're supposed to be my crew."

"The name's Shade," I said. "Tell them my name is Winston Shade."

Twenty-Three

Fred dropped me off at the Staniel Cay Yacht Club. He suggested that when we meet again, it should be under better circumstances. He planned to leave for Nassau as soon as the detective allowed him to go. He would call the FBI once he found out if Taylor was alive or dead. I gave him Jimi's cell number. We wished each other luck.

After a few beers in the bar, I found an abandoned building near the yacht club where I could spend the night. The accommodations were less than comfortable, but I was out of the rain. During the brief periods when I nodded off, all I could see in my mind was the image of Holly crying into her hands. It had been a terrible way for us to part. I could only hope that she'd pull herself together quickly, and that Jimi would step up to the plate. At least they had a bed to sleep in.

I was rousted in the morning by an employee of the yacht club. I gave him twenty bucks to take me to the airport in his golf cart. The little airline had no problem accepting cash for a ride to Fort Lauderdale. Upon landing, I found that none of the airlines or car rental companies would accept cash. How was I supposed to get back to my boat? I sat in the lobby and considered my options. I picked up a discarded newspaper and thumbed through it. I arrived at the classified section when an idea hit me. I scanned the used cars until I found what I was looking for.

Someone local was trying to sell an old Hyundai for a thousand bucks. I called the seller for directions. I hailed a cab outside. The cab driver had no problem taking my cash. The seller didn't either. I talked him down to eight hundred and drove off in my new beater. It had over two hundred thousand miles on it, but the air conditioning blew cold and everything seemed to work. The only problem was the horrible scraping noise it made when I hit the brakes. I didn't care. I only needed it to stay together until I got back to Palm Island Marina. I didn't take the time to transfer the title. I didn't even think about insurance. I just drove it hard to the west coast. I parked it in the visitor's section of the marina parking lot, and left the keys in the ignition.

Holly was heavy on my mind, but it sure was good to see *Leap of Faith* floating in her slip. Whatever happened to me, as long as I had my trusty trawler, I'd be okay. I checked the bilge for excess water. I checked the batteries. I opened her up so the salon and bunks could air out. Other than a noticeable layer of dust, everything seemed to be in order. I'd made it back to my boat before Holly and Jimi could have possibly made it back to Florida. I didn't need to be in a hurry, but I started planning for my departure. As soon as I loaded up with provisions and topped off with water and diesel, I'd leave for the Keys.

Jimi would have to get back to his boat eventually, but that was his problem. It was Holly I was worried about. I'd leave his phone inside his boat before I left, but in the meantime, I held onto it. I didn't want to miss a call from Captain Fred. I wanted to know if Taylor made it or not. I wanted her to live. I wanted her to live so that she could realize how she'd finally been thoroughly defeated by a piece of trawler trash like me. I wanted her to know that I had won. She could curse my name for the rest of her days, as long as it was from a jail cell.

It took three days, but I finally got the call. I was washing the boat when I heard the phone ring. I had to run to catch it before it quit ringing.

"That you, Breeze?" asked Captain Fred.

"Yea, it's me," I answered. "Is she alive?"

"She's alive and talking," he said.

"Did you call the FBI?" I asked.

"I did," he said. "They've been here to speak with Taylor. They'll be taking her back to the states when she's well enough to travel."

"Good news," I said.

"Maybe not," he said. "Not for you anyway."

"What's going on, Fred?"

"I told you she was talking," he said. "She's talking plenty. She fingered you as the shooter."

"What?" I screamed. "That's ridiculous."

"She told the FBI that you found her on the beach," he said. "She tried to run, but you shot her in the back."

"That's not how it went down," I told him. "You have to believe me."

"Doesn't matter what I believe," he said. "But you better get on that boat of yours and make yourself scarce. The FBI is coming for you, son."

The End

Cool Breeze Epilogue

Stephen Russell won his race for the Florida House of Representatives and became a strong voice for clean water as a basic human right.

Winston Shade disappeared from southwest Florida and was never heard from again.

Taylor Ford recovered from her gunshot wound. She was extradited back to the United States. Her trial was postponed pending a psychiatric evaluation.

Jimi D. decided that he wasn't cut out for life aboard. He sold his boat and moved to land in an undisclosed location.

Carlos Beruff lost in his primary race to Marco Rubio.

John Muller retired. He plays a lot of golf now. His friends call him "Buckets."

Captain Fred returned to Florida. *Incognito* was last seen berthed at the Pink Sands Marina, in Fort Myers Beach.

Additional Disclaimer

This is a work of fiction. The names of public figures are used fictitiously. The author claims very little knowledge of actual corruption within south Florida's judicial system. No judgement should be made as to the character of any public or private person mentioned in this book.

No political action committee by the name of Independent Florida exists.

Honorable Mention

The water quality in south Florida is a real and important issue. The author apologizes if any of the groups working to bring awareness to this problem are misrepresented. They are all doing great work. Special mention to **John Heim**, the guy on the bridge holding a sign. He's a true leader in the clean water movement.

https://www.facebook.com/groups/SWFLcleanwater/

https://www.facebook.com/evergladestrust/

https://www.facebook.com/CaptainsForCleanWater/

https://www.facebook.com/bullsugar.org/

Acknowledgements

Proofreading: Dave Calhoun

Original Cover Photo: Kim Robinson

Photo Art: Carol Chvila

Cover Design: http://ebooklaunch.com/

Interior Formatting:
http://ebooklaunch.com/

Other Books in the Series

Trawler Trash: Confessions of a Boat Bum

http://amzn.to/2bsD2N0

Following Breeze

http://amzn.to/2b4GA8X

Free Breeze

http://amzn.to/2bHHwnn

Redeeming Breeze

http://amzn.to/2b1kjH6

Bahama Breeze

http://amzn.to/2bsEq29

Other Books by Ed Robinson

Leap of Faith; Quit Your Job and Live on a Boat

http://amzn.to/2aVTGrx

Poop, Booze, and Bikinis

http://amzn.to/2b1wneA

The Untold Story of Kim

http://amzn.to/2beqOsX

Contact Ed at: kimandedrobinson@gmail.com

Visit Ed's blog at:

https://quityourjobandliveonaboat.com/

Find Ed on Facebook:

https://www.facebook.com/quityourjobandliveonaboat/

Made in the USA
Columbia, SC
04 June 2022

61316133R00174